Chrysa

By

GARY BUDGEN

Cover Art

Woman Carry An Axe
By Hyena reality

Freedigitalphotos.net

Graphics

Nathan J.D.L. Rowark

First Edition

Horrified Press

© Horrified Press

All rights reserved.
No part of this book may be used or reproduced in any manner
without written permission from the author.
All characters appearing in this work are fictitious.
Any resemblance to real persons, living or dead is purely coincidental.

ISBN: 978-1-326-79918-2

This book is dedicated to my mother Janet Lillian Budgen.

Table of Contents

Salt Cellar..5

"Salt Cellar" in *M-Brane Science Fiction* Number 26 published March 2011 Reprinted in *M-Brane Quarterly* Number 3 August 2011

Dead Countries..8

"Dead Countries" in *Where are we Going?*. an anthology from Eibonville Press (Allen Ashley ed) 2012

Lilies...16

"Lilies" *Morpheus Tales* Number 16 published April 2012

Watching Emily Dress..21

"Watching Emily Dress" in *Sein und Werden* Summer 2013

Chrysalis...24

"Chrysalis" in *Gold Dust* Issue 21 June 2012

Black Ribbon...27

"Black Ribbon" January 2014 in *Theaker's Quarterly Fiction* 46

White Goods...31

"White Goods" in *Wordland* 4. May 2014

Clown in Apus...36

"Clown in Apus" *Jupiter* Number 27 (Autonoe) published April 2010

Dawn in the Garden of England....................................55

"Dawn in the Garden of England" in *Interzone* Number 187 published March 2003

The Heart of the Labyrinth..67

"The Heart of the Labyrinth" in Issue 2 of *Body Parts*

SALT CELLAR

Because you love me you are going to have to kill me and eat me. You mustn't be sorry. I would not have you being sorry. I would not have it any other way.

This morning I watched Neptune rising, blue, flecked with ice geysers, like the pupil in the eye of a god with a stigma. It had seemed magnificent once. I waited before I turned, knowing that once I did, once I saw you, the glory before me would shrink to insignificance. I had come to Triton for the awe of the outer planets, and found instead the intimacy of your embrace.

So I turn and look. You are atop the hillside that I think of as our place. The great dome of your carapace fills the short horizon. Your shell is the blackest void, sucking in light, pulling the stars to it. Then you touch me with your mind as you have done every day since we found each other. Sometimes you have granted me visions of your home world, light years away, the liquid metal oceans and cities that rise up in crystalline knots. But today it will be past lovers. It will be a lesson.

Your courtship is majestic, a work of art. When the final moment comes your mates give up their psyche to you and you both rise through the ice beauties of n-dimensional mathematics. There is a moment of communion. Their philosophies, theories, memories and pleasures will be passed onto your children. And when you are seeded you feel the urge don't you? If you were to deny it you would die. It's all right. I understand. It is an itch that can only be scratched in one way because however godlike you are your children need physical as well as spiritual nourishment. So in ecstatic misery you consume the bodies of your lovers.

And I am sitting in a café in the East End of London near my studio and Stephen is telling me that he is leaving.

"Your work," he says.

His eyes are puffy where he has been crying or drinking too much or both. He tells me he can't compete, that he always feels second best. Even as I try to reassure him that it isn't so, part of my mind is focused on the oddly shaped salt-cellar that when he has left I will steal and use of part of my sculpture.

You love this about me don't you? It is something you could never get from one of your own. The little details of a human life are seasoning on the vaster dish that is your higher understanding. When I remember Earth, my old life, it fills you with pleasure. A rush of psychic feedback floods back into me. I run up our hill, towards you and you hold me in the great girders of your mandibles. I look into your jaws and the infinite depths beyond. Will it be now? I want it to be now.

"What is it?" Stephen asked.

We are standing before the sculpture. My most important sculpture. It is weeks before the final break up in the café.

"It is a shadow."

That is the only way to explain why I have had to do what I have. I have gone mad for a while, chasing shadows, thinking that the city itself casts one; believing that I can find it by scouring the skips, the bins and gutters for the pieces of it. If I collected enough would I not be able to see the real shape? So far I had constructed a thing that lacks symmetry, which is without form.

"It's ugly," Stephen says, smiling.
"Go away Stephen."
"You used to like me being honest about your work."
But I am already ignoring him and looking though the object catching a glimpse of what casts the shadow.

You move with such precision all your multiple legs rising and falling in an intricate rhythm as though the most perfect engineering. At first I would feel vaguely perverted like one of those oily-smelly old men who prefer pistons and flywheels, railway engines, to human beings.

But that is only shadow and you will let me see the shape itself. Now the time has come for you to eat me and I am filled with your inner darkness. It is so intense it is like light. I begin to see all you know: folded space, curled dimensions lying dormant since creation, the life cycle of stars seen all at once as tracks through space-time. Am I eaten yet? Is there more? I am in a cathedral that is larger than the universe....

But then there is a flaw, a stain of outer light that seems to rip everything away. There is one last vision, and it is me. I am seeing me as you see me and it is not small, not insignificant. I am like a little jewel you have coveted for a time, a little jewel you don't want to break.

Stephen is speaking to me for the first time; standing next to me in the gallery in Shoreditch, not knowing it is my sculpture.

"What do you think?" I ask, wanting a coo of approval even though this is an early effort, my own blood dancing in oil, trying to form a solid shadow.

"I'm not sure I get it," he says and glances at me, more interested in me than the sculpture, which annoys me, pleases me.

"Well three dimensional objects cast two dimensional shadows," I say as though reciting, but it is only an inner card I read from. "So a four dimensional object will cast a 3D shadow, apparently..."

But he has turned away from it, looking at me, appreciating me.

"You want to run that past me again," he says laughing, knowing. "Over a coffee."

And I let him lead me away with one last regretful glance at my work, my failure.

I am sat beside you on our hillside on Triton and I am alone. Your carapace is dull, and you are still. You are a dead thing now, not vital just archaeology.

I don't know how long I sit. Neptune is setting and in the last blue glow I think about the ship for the first time in ages. Then I move and look at you, and I see your final gift: the steel-taunt tendons of your legs, your intricate mandibles, the plates and sections of your exoskeleton.

I see myself tearing them away from your body. I see myself dragging them to the ship and returning with them to Earth.

I see myself beginning to work again.

DEAD COUNTRIES

I liked dead countries. It was the possibility of completion that attracted me, the thought that I would be able to get every issue without the worry of having to keep up with all the new stuff. It's funny what you get into when you're a kid.

Eric who lived across the street was more of a general collector but one day he came over to my house to show me something. I answered the front door and saw his mum across the street, making sure he crossed the road safely even though there were hardly ever any cars round our way then. He nodded to me and scratched at his acne covered forehead. When we got into my room he showed me the stamps. They were a set of commemoratives showing smiling faces in cosmonauts helmets with a rocket ship blazing in the background. The larger writing looked like angular Arabic but there was an English translation. "Heroes of the Our Space Program." The name of the country was confirmed in capitals. Quassia.

"Where's Quassia?" I asked. I had never heard of it.

Dear Francis.

Getting here has not been easy. Not everyone is allowed to make the journey. It has taken me a long time to be ready.

At the border I was questioned.

-Had I ever worked for a bank or in the stock market?

-Had I ever been a boss or fired someone from a job?

-Had I ever willingly trod on an ant?

Since they let me through everyone has been very friendly. I have had to join an official tour since they don't let foreigners just wander around getting the wrong idea and spreading even more vile propaganda.

The hotel is basic but decent enough. Tomorrow we are going on a coach tour to the launch sites of the space missions. The space program has been discontinued now. Apparently there are other priorities.

My favourite dead country was Latvia. I almost had a complete set of Latvian stamp. The first issued were just after the First World War and because of a paper shortage were printed on the back of old German Army field maps. I collected as many as possible of the 5 Kapeika values and would turn them over and try to find matching bits of the map. It felt as though I was reconstructing the landscape of this forgotten country.

The last issues were overprints of Russian stamps from just after the Soviet invasion of 1940.

Every Saturday I would go to the dealers in Peckham and see what I could afford out of my pocket money. Eric would be there sometime, his mum hovering in a corner since she wouldn't let him come on his own.

When I hadn't seen him for a while I went over to his house. He was getting more and more obsessed with Quassia.

Antiquities of Southern Quassia showing the Mausoleum of the Kings.

Famous writers of Quassia.
Butterflies.
Birds.

I looked up Quassia in the encyclopaedia at school. Nothing. I checked the big atlas with a magnifying glass looking for it tucked away in some intersection of borders near Czechoslovakia, Hungary, Yugoslavia, East Germany. Then I checked South America thinking it might be near one of those countries I could never place in my mind Paraguay, Ecuador.

I realised it must be a dead country and maybe I would have got into it if I'd carried on with stamp collecting but I was growing up, getting other interests.

Dear Francis

The achievements of Quassian engineering are really something that must be seen to be believed. Elena our guide, a beautiful young woman, is so full of enthusiasm it is contagious. Today the tour party walked for miles along the top of the Albertine Damn which provides electricity for most of the capital. It is so tall that the mighty river below looks like little more than a stream.

The damn will be mothballed soon because, as Elena explained, hydroelectric power is now obsolete. They are very big on the environment here and everyone is full of hope for the future.

By the time I was fifteen I was taking the weekend's first speed at about seven o'clock on a Friday evening. There was a whole scene. We'd listen to Horizon radio for the jazz-funk then head somewhere local or up west to the Empire or the Lyceum. The river boat discos were the best. The boat would go up and down the Thames and we'd all be dancing, while the reflections of the law courts and ministries would dance with us on the water. There was nothing better than going past the Houses of Parliament and doing a line of speed as a salute to the powers that be.

One day I went over to Eric's.

"Still into stamps?" I teased.

"Not just stamps Francis," he was straight faced. "I've been collecting photographs and books. I even get the Quassian newspaper delivered. The language isn't difficult once you've mastered the letters."

A few weeks later I took my stamp collection into the dealers. He'd always been friendly when I'd come in as a kid. I wanted money because there was an all-nighter coming up and I needed a ticket and some of this wicked sulphate that was going round.

When he finally handed over the cash it was much less than I thought the whole of Latvia was worth but I just pocketed it.

Then I blurted out: "You have anything from Quassia?"

He didn't do more than glance up from my album which he was mentally splitting into different lots.

"You've got your money son," he said, "now get out."

Dear Francis

Elena has taken me to meet her parents. It is wonderful here in the southern province where the farmlands are broken by dense forests and the legends of wolf-men and witches live on as ironic fairy tales. Elena and I go for long walks there, in the dark caves of leaves it feels like we are entering another world. I think I am falling in love.

Sometimes I would go round to Eric's house just because I had no-where else to go now. He had stayed on at school, still taken there every day by his mum. I was on the dole.
"Look at this Francis," he would say and show me album after album.
Wild Flowers of Quassia.
Ancient Churches of Quassia.
Notable Kite Makers of Quassia.
"Where do you get all this stuff?"
"I have pen-friends."
I had to remind myself that there was no Quassia. That Eric was probably making all this with stencils and letterset.

Dear Francis,
Elena assures me that after our marriage applying for citizenship will be a formality. I know now that my decision to stay here is the right one. There is optimism about this country that is completely lacking in our own.
Young people, far from being the cynical pariahs we know, feel they are part of a great collective project. While in England there is only unemployment or a hum-drum job here there is hope and optimism.

I was living in a squat in one of the big estates up near the Elephant and Castle. It wasn't far from the terraced streets where I'd grown up but felt like nothing like those.
The people there believed in a world without property or money. It was a statement to them to live like this. They were all poets or musicians or artists or revolutionaries. I didn't understand what they were talking about a lot of the time but they had electric guitars and basses. When the music throbbed through me I knew I was free.
If I went back home for the occasional Sunday roast I'd usually have to smoke a couple of joints and down a brew just to be able to handle my Mum and Dad.
"How's Eric?"
"Got a place at university but never went," my Mum said and touched her head.
"Another bloody waster," said my Dad.

Dear Francis,
For our honeymoon we visited the eastern lakes and the ancient monuments on the shores around them. I saw the ruins that I once glimpsed on postage stamps so long ago. The Mausoleum of the Kings is built almost to a different scale to a normal building, as though made for a race of giants.

I wandered through it hand in hand with my beautiful new wife and pondered the decay of civilizations. Elena gently chided me about this melancholy. Civilizations decline because they neglect their most important resource: the well-being of the people.

This evening we dined in the hotel restaurant, simple and appetising fare. We looked out over the ruins and as the sun set they became only shadows without power, without threat.

I did horse for a while. We liked to call it horse in our crowd, we were romantics. I didn't have the balls for hard-core addiction so I settled for booze and pills and fags. Very mundane but still cost a bit. Then I was caught in HMV pushing CDs down the front of my trousers. It's a wonderful thing progress; I'd never have got a vinyl album down there.

I wasn't banged up because my Mum and Dad agreed to have me back which was good of them considering I was a right cunt.

There was nothing to do now, round where I'd grown up. I used to sit at my bedroom window smoking. Sometimes I'd see Eric's silhouette at his own window. One day I went over and knocked.

Eric's Mum answered.

"Oh Francis," she was so glad to see me, a novel experience in those days, "won't Eric be delighted."

I went up to his room. He had a computer now and sat staring into the black screen with its green letters. His hair hung down in clumps to his shoulders and he had a ginger Jesus beard. He was in a dressing gown and the room smelt vaguely of disinfectant, semen and damp.

"Hello Francis," he said as if he'd only seen me the day before, "I'm just FTPing some documents from the mainframe of Quassia University."

"Still into all that?"

I looked around the room. Apart from the bed every surface was covered with books, notepads, stamp-albums and those long trains of perforated paper from the computer's printer. There were drawings and hand-drawn maps pinned to the walls.

"I'm studying the technological innovations that are going on there. I've become quite an expert. There aren't many in the field."

"I'll bet."

The door bumped open and Eric's mum stood there with a tray with a jug of orange squash and two beakers. There was little plate with biscuits arranged around it in a circle.

"What do you want?" Eric said.

"I just... I just..." she stammered and entered the room. She looked around for a place to put the tray and hesitated for a moment over the bed, then just stood there till I got up and took it from her.

"Thank you Francis," she said.

I thought she would go then. Eric was glaring at her but she just stood there.

"I was wondering," she said at last, "why you two boys don't go out, for a walk or something."

Eric had turned back to his computer and was tapping away.

"Yeah," I said, "we could go down the pub." I reckoned she would bung us a few quid.

"Oh I'm allowed to go out without my mum am I now?" Eric said without turning. "And Francis I don't go to pubs. I don't want to end up being a degenerate like you. Then I'd never get into Quassia."

Dear Francis,

It is with reluctance that we have left the East and our honeymoon. We took the high-speed maglev back to the capital where I am to take up my post at the university this autumn. Elena wants to make sure the apartment is comfortable for us before I start work.

They held up my dole money on some technicality so I started taking the odd fiver from my Mum's purse and the Toby jug at the back of the food cupboard where they kept the emergency money.

When they kicked me out I managed to take my Mum's charm bracelet and the watch my Granddad had left my Dad; it would have been mine one day anyway.

Some part of me knew I was breaking their hearts but mostly I just wanted a drink.

As I walked out the door I saw Eric up at his window. He waved at me.

"Prick," I said waving back.

Dear Francis,

I'm sorry it's been so long since I've written. The work at the university has kept me busy and the arrival of my twin sons has occupied all my spare time.

The project I have been involved in has borne great results. An artificial forest now covers most of the capital and my designs for energy capturing leaves have won for me great respect in society; not that there is the accompanying celebrity and excessive wealth that I hear is now such an affliction in Europe and North America.

What is most important is that we have been able to harness the energy of the sun and provide clean and almost limitless power. The trees themselves are, if I say so myself, very beautiful, like great sculptures of quartz and silver forming a canopy over our heads.

Without the need to pay excessive costs for power the price of most goods in Quassia has fallen to a level where no-one need live in scarcity. Work can be directed toward useful social projects rather than just meeting basic needs.

There were a few rough years. I was never entirely on the streets, not for more than a few days anyway. Mostly I was in squats but the people were different now, harder; everything was done because they had to do it. There were no dreams about a better world.

The laws must have changed because we were getting thrown out more often.

I was in a house up near Waterloo. The streets were Victorian terraces being renovated by people who had somehow made shed-loads in shares and privatisation.

There were two other people in the house: a bloke and some girl. They used to moan about me using their food. They put food colouring in the milk to make it look like blood; as if that would stop me.

One night the landlord's two heavies smashed in the front door and starting chucking our stuff out the window into the rain. The other people in the squat, the bloke and the girl, seemed to have somewhere they could go. As they walked away from me it was turning dark and the rain was getting heavier. I realised I hardly knew them at all. I got lost wandering those costume drama set streets until I found one of those upmarket off-licenses that sell mostly wine. I treated myself to a bottle of vodka and some cider.

When I found a shop doorway I huddled down just in the shadow out of the yellow glare of the street light. I looked into the shop window through the diamond security mesh and realised it was a stamp dealer. It was the first time I'd seen one in years. There was something reassuring about the card mounts with their stamps. I saw some Latvian ones and was suddenly confused. There were the ones with the little bits of maps on the back; there were others that I recognised. But then there were a whole load that were new to me and I'd known every Latvian stamp there was. I started to laugh. They'd resurrected Latvia hadn't they? I'd heard something about it somewhere.

Then I saw it. Picked out by the yellow light was a single stamp on a card mount of its own. It had a hand-written label saying "Very Rare £50". It showed the silhouette of a city with elegant towers. It bore the unmistakable name: Quassia.

Dear Francis
You really must visit us sometime. The capital is more magnificent than ever. The artificial forest is now complemented by a real forest. These trees are able to absorb excessive carbon and other greenhouse gases and turn them into a hard but malleable wood that forms our main building material. The city is becoming a new Eden but one in which the inhabitants have already rejected temptation.

My Mum and Dad's house was dark but I wasn't interested in that right now. Eric's bedroom light was on, and from the street I could see the flicker of a computer screen.

I found a pebble in his front yard and threw it up. My aim was pretty good given how much I'd had to drink. Eric opened the window and stuck his head out of the window. He was so hairy he looked like Captain Caveman.

"Oh it's you Francis," he said, "you'd better come up."

A downstairs light came on and then Eric led me in. As I stumbled along the corridor his Mum appeared in the kitchen door, I wondered where the tray with the orange squash was.

Eric had a different computer now. The screen was full of colour and there were images of forests and animals and crowds of people. He went over to it and clicked something and the screen changed to black with a swirling pattern. I stared at it and followed the movements for a moment.

"I've seen something," I said.

"What have you seen Francis?"

And what was it? Through the wire mesh, through the glass in a display lit only by sickly yellow light. It danced in my head, one inch by half an inch, the silhouette of a city.

"I've seen Quassia."

He made me explain.

I begged for booze, anything and he brought a bottle of sherry that had never been opened. He made me say everything again even as I grew even drunker propped up against the headboard of his bed.

The last thing I remember was his urgent hissing.

Are you sure? Are you sure?

Dear Francis,

It is all arranged. Your entry visa and papers have been organised and there is an open ticket for transit available that you can activate for the date that suits you best.

You can live in Quassia as you like and you will want for nothing. You could even decide to do nothing but I'm sure at some point you'll want to get involved in one of the projects. The field trips into the new forests are very rewarding. You get to catalogue the species that are evolving there. It's a bit like stamp collecting really, only much more rewarding.

So when you are ready I'll be waiting. Just find your way to the consulate and the rest is easy.

My head was run through with waves of pain and each wave frothed with nausea. I'd wet myself.

I'd had plenty of mornings like this.

A man stood over me. He was about my age with closely cropped hair and clean shaven. Even through the stench of my own piss he smelt fresh and perfumed. He was carrying a small leather valise. It was some moments before I realised.

"Eric?"

"There's a glass of water there," he pointed to the bedside table.

I tried to sit up and just about managed it.

"What's going on?"

"I hope you feel better soon. I've got to be going now."

I managed to get out of bed and followed him out of the bedroom. I reached the top of the stairs as he reached the bottom.

"Eric," I said, "where are you going?"

Then his Mum appeared and silently, without fuss, she helped him get into a long woollen coat.

Eric kissed her on the forehead and looked up at me.

"I'll write," he said.

Then he was gone and his mother was already coming up the stairs tears in her eyes.

"You can borrow some of Eric's clothes," she said as she hustled me back into the bedroom.

"Sure," I said, "yeah. I should be getting over the road, make my peace."

"What do you mean?"

"My Mum and Dad."

Her face went pale and she made me sit on the bed while she sat next to me. They were dead of course: Dad going quickly after Mum a couple of years before. No-one had known where I was.

"You have a bath and get changed, and I'll make a nice cup of tea. You can stay here for a bit."

I had no-where to go. I looked around the room, at the piles of typescripts, at the hand-drawn maps pinned above the desk, at the bookshelf full of stamp-albums and scrap books. It was all here. And one day Eric would write.

LILIES

A distant radio station hissed and between the static was a voice claiming to be one of the living. Then a rhythmic clanking from the scullery interrupted me. I had left my keys in the trousers I had put into the washing machine and the lining of the drum had torn; so it was I came to fall in love with one of the damned.

The indignity of having to trudge shivering through the snow to a working-class neighbourhood and enter the public laundrette was compensated when I saw her for the first time. Amid the stench of sweat and detergent I was struck immediately by her difference from the other women there. They were laughing bags of blotched skin and fat pressed into colourful frocks, but she was calm and graceful in a simple black dress, her skin white and flawless. Like alabaster I had told myself having only the vaguest idea of what alabaster was.

"Your machine broken down too citizen?" I asked smiling, knowing that someone in her station could not have afforded a washing machine but wanting the attention of those black eyes. I was trying not to stare at her breasts or the bundle of plain white underwear in her laundry basket that I found so alluring in its simplicity.

"I have no machine," she said, "I'm afraid I must come here often. Once a week. At just this time."

She had only the odd musical accent of twenty streets or so away.

We didn't say anything after that but exchanged eye smiles from either end of the long gallery that formed the launderette. When she left she turned and smiled fully as she revealed her name. Irena.

Over the next few days I tried to get on with my job. I didn't want to be infatuated with one of the damned. The very presence in our part of the city of their émigré colony was considered suspect. They were even regarded by some to be a fifth-column come to infiltrate and corrupt those of us who were alive. Those suspicions were typical of the character of that era of phoney war when only the odd street would occasionally change hands, would fall to them and become dead. The undercurrent of paranoia formed part of the rationale of my own work monitoring broadcasts from distant cities. It was believed that life might still exist somewhere else, beyond the wide expanses of the dead, and that we might find allies there.

But now I found it hard now to concentrate on my work.

I paced around.

I looked up 'alabaster' in my antique etymology. Hydrous sulphate of calcium. White, almost translucent. Used to fashion the effigies on tombs in the era when such edifices had been necessary. Oh yes.

I didn't telephone and ask for a repairman to call. The washing machine lay idle and within a week I had another pile of dirty clothes to take to the launderette. She was there, at the far end again and when there was no one too near her I left my machine and went and sat next to her.

"How long have you been here?" I asked.

"A little while. Not long." She only looked at me when she had finished speaking.

"I meant," I said, realizing that I might have been misunderstood, "how long have you been on this side of the city."

She laughed for a moment but it was little more than a whisper of air. "Who are you? Are you a spy?"

"My name is M." I said, telling her my full name, "and yes I'm a spy. I have to keep watch on people like you because there are people here who see a kind of purity in the grey militarism of your part of the city."

I had started off trying to be humorous but realised that it hadn't come out like that, that I had uttered a thought I'd never articulated before.

"I'm sorry," I said, "I didn't mean to offend you, trying to be clever, trying to impress you…" I felt myself blush, and was then ashamed at such a blatant display of my healthy blood flow.

"It's all right," she said, "I forgive you."

A few weeks later Irena was staying over in my house a few nights a week and then moved in leaving the room she rented above the grocers where she worked. She wouldn't give up the job though, despite my insisting that I could support us both.

I would quite happily spend an evening just looking at her, holding her cold and immaculate hand in mine as we sat on the sofa with the sound of the television down. Outside the snow would be falling on the streets in a rhythm that I like to think formed a wall that enclosed and protected us. Of course we always fell to touching, kissing. Before we fucked on the floor Irena would always switch off the television and plug in the little two-bar electric heater before taking off her clothes. I wondered if she felt the cold or if this was for my benefit although I always kept my shirt on. Naked she became an animated creature of marble that I felt deliciously profane in ravishing. That she was incapable of climaxing only made me want to conquer her more, although sometimes, afterwards, I could despise her for it.

One Saturday I took her to Autocue Boulevard, parading along with her in the snow flecked fur coat I had bought her and insisted she wear. I did not care about the looks we got. We passed boutiques displaying the latest fashions but every time I asked if she wanted to go in she said, no, that's all right. I insisted that we enter Skinner and Loves Department Store where I assured her everything and anything could be had. The common wisdom was that the dead of all types came to this part of the city to get the designer clothes, shoes and gadgets that could not be had on their side but Irena showed no interest at all.

We wandered among the showroom of flowing dresses and couture, the lingerie department with its abundance of ruffled lace and silk resembling flowers overflowing in a hothouse. With her perfect skin I knew I could make her more beautiful than even the mannequins. But she would not consent.

When we got back to the house I found I was irritated by this act of resistance, and the more I tried to dismiss this feeling, tried to revel in the pleasure of just being with her that had sustained me for so many weeks, the more I found I was snapping at her.

"I don't understand why you came here Irena, I don't understand why you escaped in the first place."

She looked at me and her face was still so that she could, for a moment, have been mistaken for a statue. She would speak then, I told myself, she will say something about enjoying her job in the grocers where she met other émigrés; if I was lucky she might even say that she enjoyed being with me.

"Escape?" she said at last, "we come here but it is not escape. We are the damned because of what we have done in life. You want to know what it is that I did? You will not ask me but you want to know. The truth is I can't tell you, not definitely. That is part of our torment. Sometimes I remember a child and I am putting a cigarette out on her arm and she looks back at me and the look of betrayed love rips apart something inside. Then, suddenly, I know that I never did such a thing, that there was just a moment when I thought of doing it and that was enough. On other occasions I am the child thinking back on what was done to me, examining the burns on my arm and these are just a part of what made me a monster. To become one of the damned the act is not necessarily something great. A trivial act of unkindness might be enough. Perhaps it is not even the act itself but something about the act. It could be that neither the child nor the woman is me but that I knew them and did nothing."

By the time she finished I had my head in my hands.

"Please Irena…" I began.

I did not look up. I did not want her to see that I was not crying, that I was irritated that I had never even thought about why she had been damned.

"It is all right M.," she said, "I forgive you."

Then she stood up and went over to the television and turned it on. The sound was down but we could both see what was happening. It was a news report from the other part of the city, a military parade among the damned, an endless procession of grey uniforms and armoured cars flowing like a centipede over a snow-covered street churning the white purity into an ashen morass.

I threw myself into my work and tried to forget how much I had upset her. But it was difficult because most of the clearer broadcasts seemed to have suddenly ceased. All I could pick up that purported to be from the living were voices so distant that their messages were garbled into nonsense by interruption and static.

One day Irena came home with flowers. A customer at the grocers, another émigré woman, had brought them for her as a thank you for some small kindness that Irena had performed.

The flowers were white lilies.

I said nothing, unable to openly shatter her joy. Irena fussed in arranging the flowers, finally clapping her hands together like a child as she regarded them. She had placed them on the table that stood in the bay window where they might get some of the meagre light that came from outside.

The waxy pearl skin of the leaves glowed.

I couldn't bring myself to ask her if she knew that white lilies were associated with death. They were the funeral flowers given to relatives when someone here died and passed over to that other part of the city.

The next day the television news reported that one of the periodic purges was underway among the damned. There were round-ups at night and public show trials, exhortations to greater productivity of guilt. I could see that Irena was upset.

She stood in the bay windows, in the bracket of enfolding light her back to the snowfall outside. The lilies must have opened since the day before because their scent had begun to fill the room. She caressed one of the curved leaves with a finger that was as white as the lily itself. As she stroked the leaves it looked to me almost as if she were fussing over a pet.

"Oh why can't we just learn to love the things we have left? Why must they have it their own way? We suffer enough for what we have done but they always want more, always more. And never any forgiveness."

She bent and sniffed the lilies, drawing their perfume into her and savouring it as though it were a communication that she could decipher.

So the smell of the lilies grew and this, of course, was something that I couldn't stand. To me it filled the house with an overpowering sweetness that was somehow both rotten and at the same time antiseptic, artificial. I really didn't know how long I'd be able to put up with it. How long did flowers last? Days? Over a week?

It had begun to affect my ability to concentrate on the ever more broken broadcasts on my radio. Despite their lack of coherence it was still my job to transcribe them but it reached the point when the stench of the lilies was so strong that I sat for two hours and all I had been able to understand were two fragments:

<u>Cherish everything.</u>
<u>Art is no substitute.</u>

I turned on the television to distract myself. The leadership committee of the damned had issued a statement. They were outraged that those on the living side of the city had dared comment on their latest purge. There was fighting talk, more parades of soldiers and missile launchers down the bleak central avenue of that part of the city. It frightened me and I wanted to forget it, to get on with my work, but here I was drowning in the overpowering emanations of the lilies.

From beneath the sink I took out a bottle of bleach. I took the lilies from the vase and emptied the water down the sink watching it trickle away. Then I poured a healthy dose of bleach into the vase and then immersed the lilies in it.

By the following evening the leaves had browned and curled. Irena was upset. Her fingers now stroked as though she might impart some life into the flowers but she had no life in her to give.

The television was on showing the public trial of some of the damned for disloyalty to the regime. The tone of our newsreader though was not condemnatory as might have expected, but rather it was as though our side of the city was making excuses, trying to placate the damned.

Irena bent to examine the lilies.

"It is terrible," she said, "how little time things last. How fragile a beautiful moment is."

The next morning when she left for work she was back almost immediately.

"There is something wrong," she said, "the streets are quiet. Many shops are shut. My shop is shut."

We watched the news all day, turning the television off so I could fuck her on the sofa, on the floor, over a chair. She cried often. I wanted to cry, I really did, but there was nothing I could precisely fix on that would allow me to do so.

When evening came we went to bed early.

Then in the small hours something awoke me. It was not a gradual awakening but a coming to complete consciousness in one instant. Numbness had come over me as though I was immersed in a viscous liquid. I couldn't even feel the usual chill of the night.

I crept downstairs and without stopping to inspect them I took the lilies from the vase. In the kitchen I ran the stems under running water from the tap. I poured the milky bleach down the plughole and then washed the vase carefully. Finally I filled the vase with fresh water and put the lilies back into it. I then placed them back in the curve of the bay windows amid the feeble glow from the streetlights outside.

But it was too late. The leaves were now wrinkled like ancient parchment or a discarded cocoon. The smell of the lilies had entirely gone.

I turned on the television but instead of the all night news bulletins there was nothing but static and a message saying that normal service would be resumed as soon as possible.

Then, from outside I heard the contented growl of a diesel engine and the march of many feet. Searchlights dazzled my living room.

Irena stood behind me on the stairs. It was as if I had never seen her naked before. The searchlights marked highlights and depressions across her body so that she was transfigured, clothed in some vital new skin, no longer the gentle white of alabaster, of lilies, but an angry glare, migraine white, as white as faith.

As I pulled the curtain and net back to look outside I knew what it was that I would see. A wind was swirling the snowflakes around in a frenzied dance. In the street there were armoured cars and either side of them the columns of grey uniformed soldiers looking straight ahead, not needing to inspect the houses that they marched past, expecting no resistance from anyone here.

This was now their home.

WATCHING EMILY DRESS

My habit of watching Emily get dressed in the morning, once something she appreciated, had grown slowly into something else, perhaps found disturbing, a reverse metamorphosis, a butterfly thought into a maggoty little obsession. It began with that, the image of her bending her leg slightly to put her foot into her underwear, almost like a ballerina who has just lifted a foot from the floor as she attempts passé. And all day, when Emily was out at work, that image multiplied in my inner hall of mirrors, my compound mind. From the bed I looked across the room. It was so clean, so hygienic. It was nothing like the filthy pit we stayed in near the Gare du Nord. That had been full of cockroaches and I had watched Emily dress, a show for me then, my look appreciated after we had made love amidst the filth and morning sunlight.

Then I saw it across this too clean bedroom: one solitary skirting-board warrior, a ground beetle.

"Hello, little ronin," I said.

Already I was not quite human.

It was the day after I'd found the ground beetle, now suffocated in a matchbox in the bedside cabinet. I did manage to get up that day. Made it all the way to the library where the closing down sale was still going on. There were a few popular books. Nothing like the text books I had once had. I tried not to remember the days I had spent with them on a blanket in Brick Lane market. Another academic selling off books: old review copies, inspection copies. I was lucky I suppose, at least books on entomology have some good colour plates. I watched designer city couples; thinking they were daring going further east than Spitalfields, rip out pictures for framing: dragonflies, whirligigs and damselflies all to go on a toilet wall or forgotten hallway. I found the books in the gutter.

So, I came back from the library with my penny purchases and laid them out on the bed, six: one for each leg. I was constructing a machine that would effect my transformation.

It wasn't the whole Gregor Samsa trip that I wanted no. Not to be disgusting. More like Jeff Goldblum in The Fly (1986). The image where Geena Davis takes off her stocking and sends it through the teleporter was the sort of scene that could haunt me all day if I allowed it. Even as an insect Jeff was sexy. That might get some interest. That might get Emily into bed. It might even get me out of bed.

The next morning Emily loomed over me.

"What are you going to do today?"

"I don't know...."

"You can't just give up."

She was smartly dressed, for the office. Short black skirt etc. I liked that, the distance it put between us made her even more desirable.

"No," I said, "you're right."

From where I lay I reached out with my antennae to touch her. I ran them along her flanks just above the hips, nothing lewd but, rather, affectionate. She didn't feel a thing, just left to go to work.

I must have lain there all day; absorbing structures, their sounds making little poems in my head: scutum, scutellum, elytra...scutum, scutellum, elytra. Then she was standing over me, still in her smart suit, her hair come slightly untangled, falling from its slides in an utterly delicious way.

She waved some papers.

"There's a job," she said, "I've printed it all off for you...."

I looked at her, multiple images, a giant about to reach over and pluck me up, put me in a matchbox. Did I wince? The look of disappointment across her faces wounded me.

"What is it?" I said.

"Well, it's just a general admin job..."

We could live in filth amid cockroaches in Paris, couldn't we? Did it all matter so much, the endless scrambling around to maintain a life-style?

"You'll have to lie," she said.

"Why?"

"Because you're massively over-qualified."

"Then, I'll lie."

"That's the spirit."

And she leant over and kissed me, kissed the hardening chitin of my carapace, her touch so rare it made me shudder, almost piss myself, almost die.

The questions were baffling.

Discuss a situation in which you have shown initiative.

How have you demonstrated team work in your current stroke last position?

I tried to answer, watching the ink crawl over the page in letters and words, aphids of meaning that were beginning to seem meaningless. Afterwards I scuttled to a corner and found a silverfish to crunch on before I fell asleep.

I was on the ceiling when she brought the good news.

"You've got an interview."

I was looking down at her, could see just inside her blouse, to the curve of her breasts. I could leap down and ravish her; and in my multiple visions it would be replayed out to an infinity, a lovemaking as decadent as any mirrored fin de siècle brothel of the imagination.

"Well," she said, "it's brilliant isn't it?"

Take off your clothes, I wanted to cry. You are a human and I can only worship you. I am only fit to be crushed beneath the heel of your shoe. But please take off your clothes.

"Yes," I said, "it's brilliant."

The office complex was vast, filled with tunnels and cavities, a nest of scampering life that I could almost feel at home in. I was sat at a table with two people on the other side, a woman with a wart on her cheek and a man whose hair wouldn't stay down. In my multiple vision their many forms stacked up, spread around. They seemed wary and I realised that they weren't so unlike me, that they too had potential for transformation; I imagined them as ants. Yes they would do well as ants.

I tried to answer their questions but really had no idea what it was they wanted me to say.

"I spent six years on a doctorate and ten teaching at a university."

"A what?"

"I studied insects."

They looked at each other.

"You see," said the man, "what you did doesn't really contribute to the economy does it? You can't expect people to do proper work to support those sorts of activities...."

Or rather he said nothing like that. Or meant to say it and said:

"And how would you use your experience in the role you are applying for?"

I always preferred beetles to ants. Individuals rather than neurons in a hive mind.

The next time I watched her dress her tights laddered as she pulled them up. She sat on the bed and cried, holding a leg of scrunched up hose in her hand, the other leg still on, ragged where it had torn.

"My last pair," she said, "my God, I'm crying. Crying over a pair of tights. But we've got no money."

"Maybe that job..." I began.

"That was days ago," she snarled, "don't you remember? They turned you down."

She sat for a while trying to do some trick with nail varnish to repair the tights, something she had learned from her mother.

I diminished into a corner, a small thing, small enough to hide behind a grain of dust, in awe at her vast humanity.

I watched her dress for the last time, throwing the ruined tights to the floor where they lay like an abandoned cocoon.

"I'll freeze," she said, "but at least I won't look like a tramp."

There is a type of rove beetle that secretes a sweet liquor. Ants live off it. They find the taste so irresistible that they carry the beetle with them wherever they go, feeding off the liquor. The beetle is blind, defenceless and yet it survives, protected by the ants, loved by them.

Alone, I got the matchbox from the bedside cabinet. It was now as big as a double coffin so there was room for me to lie down next to the ground beetle. I will dream here; I will recall an existence among fabulous creatures with their cars and theatre trips; I will remember giving lectures and evenings spent in restaurants and laughing in bars. I will go into the future cherishing hope, keeping close the mornings of sunlight watching Emily dress.

CHRYSALIS

He could begin his life again now that the new conservatory was complete. He wheeled himself in, away from the house with the smashed-faced television and the heavily curtained windows. In the conservatory the heat was amplified into a sub-tropical haze but the light was scattered on the surface of the panes and recombined into images set to his neural signature. At the moment it was the standard factory setting of a south sea island. But soon, as the brochure had explained, the sympathetic glass would adjust and begin to show him the idealisation of his inner desires.

He let the old woman who looked after him put plants in the corners of the conservatory. Now he would sit and absorb the heat and wait for the glass to change.

"Why did you smash the television?" the woman asked.

"Didn't like what it showed me."

"I'll get some spray for these plants; get rid of all these worms."

"They're not worms. They're caterpillars. In a few weeks they'll change..."

He imagined his future in an iridescent butterfly house the view above and around him of his idealised wishes.

The next morning he read poetry, Marvell and Donne, and the conservatory glass showed the massed leaves and branches of Epping Forest. Above the top of his book the green blur comforted him. Only once was it broken when something flitted between the trees, a flash of orange and indigo of a woman's summer dress that he recognised.

Later that afternoon the screens adjusted again and now revealed what he had suspected. It was Wendy. It was the beach at Broadstairs on their first holiday together. She strode across the sand toward him, the wind twining her sarong around her, making her, for a moment am exotic creature, deliciously serpentine.

"These worms are taking over," the woman said when she brought in his late afternoon tea.

"I've told you..."

But already she wasn't listening, adjusting the cushion at the back of his wheelchair, his atrophied legs.

"You don't have to make a fuss."

"There's nothing wrong with you. You could get up if you wished."

But he knew that his legs were brittle sticks. Last time he had tried to walk he had fallen and writhed on the floor in front of the television unable to reach the control.

Perhaps it would have been better not to spend all his time in the conservatory but the alternative was the house itself. He took to sleeping in the conservatory, in his chair with a blanket thrown over him or even managing to manoeuvre onto the couch. At night, without sunlight, the glass was opaque and in the dark he listened to the movement on the plants, the caterpillars crawling and chewing in preparation for their change.

He awoke always to Wendy filling the upper glass walls and ceiling of the conservatory. She approached from middle distance down the meadow from Glastonbury Tor, and jumped down the sand dunes of Harlech beach from the summer after. When she got nearer, her face filling whole panes, it was as though she would say something. She began to mouth the words but then the scene would shift and he would glimpse her in the distance again and all he could do was wait for her approach.

"You really must do something about these...these things," the woman bustled in, "if they aren't worms then they must be maggots. Something nasty."

He didn't want to hear; he knew what they were even if they were proving stubborn to any metamorphosis, reluctant to be reborn.

"Anyway why are you spending so much time in here? Why don't you come back into the house? You can afford a new television. I can order it..."

"No...I...I don't want to watch television. Everything's changed. Nothing makes any sense anymore."

"What do you see in those windows?"

"Go away."

It was almost as if he might hear what Wendy was saying. He strained in his chair, stretching out his neck towards the light, the scattered light that reformed into endless versions of Wendy. He needed to get nearer and venturing back into the house he found an old walking stick from their days of hiking. He managed to push himself up out of the wheelchair and stand. Closer now her lips were like gigantic bulbous pods, latent with meaning. But before he could make it out he wobbled and fell back into his wheelchair.

"I love you," he told the conservatory glass.

When the woman brought his tea he glared at her to go away. He waited for Wendy to come again and there she was sauntering down a tree lined avenue in the grounds of Audley End House. He hips swayed beneath her bright summer dress. Now she was saying something again. What is it? What is it?

He was standing now, leant on stick he could almost make it out. And his feet squished on something. The floor was covered in caterpillars.

"You're standing up!" It was the woman. Then she saw the floor, "my God all these worms."

He stared at Wendy it was almost as if he could understand.

"She's trying to tell me something," he shouted.

"Who?"

"Wendy."

"Wendy? Is that what you see up there?" The woman began to make a sort of gulping noise, the lump in her throat moving; at first he thought it was a laugh, but as she turned and fled he realised she was sobbing.

Across the floor he watched the caterpillars turning, struggling to be somewhere else.

Using his stick he climbed up onto to the sofa and managed to get his face as near as possible. Wendy's lips loomed before him the slow tearing away of one from another, the tiny strands of spittle as she mouthed the all-important message...

Then an enormous droning filled the conservatory and the woman rolled in pushing the vacuum cleaner ripping the caterpillars from the floor, churning their bodies in the wheels and rollers, destroying any potential they had to ever change.

"No," he screamed.

Before he knew what he was doing he swung the walking stick in a horizontal arc that should have hit the women in the head, should have cracked her skull, except it missed and smashed into the conservatory. The crash was spectacular, instantly short-circuiting the image. The young woman he had seen there was gone forever.

For a moment the air was filled with a flock of glass shards, they flew around for a moment as the air rushed in from outside. They caught the sunlight, multi-coloured creatures sparkling like spangles.

He climbed down from the sofa, throwing away the stick as though it had suddenly become a snake. As it clattered on the floor he went over to the woman. She leant on the vacuum cleaner, exhausted, tears rolled down her lined face. But now he could see though the mask of years.

"Wendy," he said, "you're so old."

But as he made to embrace her he had seen his own hands, wrinkled and spotted.

"Yes," she said, "yes."

BLACK RIBBON

Since the invasion of the city Isabel had worked with the black ribbon. Her office was in one of the old storage bunkers. Once, the whole complex would have offered a modicum of comfort: air conditioning, running water and overhead lighting. The storage room itself, sealed with perfect conditions for the black ribbon, was intact; but the rest of the complex had been reduced to little more than a set holes or partially covered cellars connected by closed tunnels or trenches.

Isabel's office at least had a roof, but it was a dingy place, lit by a small electric lamp running from an extension cord hooked to the generator set up by the Captain and his men. She had a desk with a Bakelite telephone and a heavy manual typewriter. Also on the desk were the various machines on which she listened to the black ribbon. There was a clock on the wall but it had stopped. The hands had set at quarter to three, the time the invasion of the city had begun. Isabel had prised the hands off, not wanting to be reminded of her people's great shame. Now the clock was just a dial with Roman numerals. She found it oddly elegant.

The Captain had brought her here personally, seating her in the chair at the desk and looming over her from the other side. His uniform was entirely black except for some silver epaulettes and the piping around them. And of course the bright silver death's head badge on his cap.

"You will transcribe," he had said.

"Why?"

"The black ribbon must be transcribed."

"All of it?"

He had just shown her the storeroom, filled with black ribbon; some of it on large reels, other—more recent—in various formats of cartridges and cassettes.

"There is no time limit," he said, and he smiled for the first time, his white skin creasing around his mouth, his eyes still dull.

"And I expect," Isabel had said, "that there is more every day."

He turned away at that, facing through the walls of the bunker towards that part of the city where the conquest was not quite complete, where there was still some stubborn resistance.

"I have been to many places," he said. "Every city is different. In some places every moment of a person's life is inscribed in microdots on the retinas of their eyes. Other cities have people who with crystals filled with hieroglyphs inside their skulls. And here, here there is the black ribbon."

Yes, the Captain had been lots of places but he didn't seem to understand that the black ribbon was sacred, never to be listened to; only to be stored in the bunkers forever. The record of vanished lives.

"And what about you?" she'd asked, "How do you keep your life?"

The Captain had looked at her for a moment.

"We are the conquerors," he said, "We do not have to answer questions."

Isabel shrugged. She looked around the desk at the various machines. Some played reels and others played cassettes or cartridges.

"Very well," she said.

"The black ribbon must be transcribed," he said again, "All life must become text. You will listen to the black ribbon and transcribe. When you have finished your task the transcription will form a great chapter in the book we will send to God."

They fed her well enough and gave her cigarettes. Sometimes, to break the relentless misery of her work she would leave the office and go up to the surface. In the distance, across the rubble, she could see the flashes of fire and plumes of smoke from the other side of the city where the battles continued.

It was on such an occasion that she saw the resistance fighter try to kill the Captain. The fighter came out of the rubble somewhere and ran at the Captain with a knife. For a moment Isabel was filled with the thrill of the Captain's imminent demise. But the Captain pulled out his automatic pistol and shot the fighter, a young boy.

Isabel watched as the Captain crouched down and undid the boy's shirt. He opened the chest cavity and pulled out one of the new format micro-cassettes that had been used in recent years.

"Here," he said handing it to Isabel, "more black ribbon."

Then she went back down beneath the ground to her office.

She worked with no particular order, taking at random from the storeroom and playing the reels or cassettes or cartridges on the relevant machines and typing up as she listened.

It took about half a day to get through each life, an average life. Dead children were much quicker and once there was a ninety-year old woman who took from morning till long into the evening.

Isabel tried not to pause when she came across some particular highlight.

-<u>My tears when I held her in my arms after she had just been born, her hair so thin it was almost not there.</u>

-<u>As I walked into the apartment that for the first time; after that riverside hovel it was so vast, like a cathedral.</u>

-<u>I know I am dying. I want to remember the verses they taught us at school.</u>

Many of the lives seemed, superficially, to be the same: growing up; the first flush of love; the disappointments of middle age; the acceptance of aging. Any yet each one had a rhythm of its own, or perhaps better to call it a flavour. Whatever it was she could not quite define it.

Isabel altered nothing, keeping the precise idioms and tense of the black ribbon recordings exactly. Some of the older reels had degraded, the magnetic particles worn away or the fixing agent so decrepit that the particles were simply no longer there at all. The lives on these old reels had become a series of fragments, odd words and phrases between white noise; but she transcribed these exactly as she heard them as well.

Then, one day, she found a black ribbon that was in a format she had not come across before. It was a large reel with a ribbon wider than would fit on any of the machines in her office. She thought of putting it aside but no; she would make the Captain work.

"I need a different machine for this," she told him, finding him on the surface looking through a pair of field-glasses.

He took the reel from her and weighed it in his hand.

"Very well," he said, "what do you require?"

"I will have to look."

He pondered this for a moment. Then he nodded.

He led her himself, through streets reduced to paths between ruins. They went through wrecked department stores where clothing hung on racks all covered with brick dust from shattered walls. She saw children's toys smashed into fragments of wood and plastic.

They found the right machine in an old radio repair shop and Isabel carried it as best she could. It was heavy and awkward and it was a long walk back to the bunker.

The attack came at dusk. Ragged resistance fighters, almost children, came at them. This time the Captain only managed to kill one before the other stuck a knife in his back.

"You're free," one of them said to Isabel.

She just stood there holding the tape machine.

"Come with us!"

"I can't," she said, "I must tend to the black ribbon."

They said nothing but nodded solemnly, recognising--as she now did--the sacred nature of her duty.

When they were gone she put down the tape machine and crouched next to the Captain. He was still alive.

"You must take it," he said.

"What?"

And he tapped his chest. She understood then that he too was from the city. That for him the invasion had been a homecoming.

"You are a traitor," she told him.

"We will all be in the book we will send to God," he said.

When he had gone she opened his chest cavity and took out a cassette in the standard format used until a decade or so ago. She pocketed this and picked up the machine and trudged back to the bunker.

In her office she set up the old machine salvaged from the radio repair shop. She placed the old reel on it and threaded the ribbon through the heads onto the counter reel. When she played it the sound was barely decipherable, mostly hiss and static interrupted by a few words she could make out here and there. She typed it all exactly as she heard it.

This then had been the fate of all those lives. Put into the bunker to preserve them into the future they would, instead, have degraded into incomprehensibility.

She placed the Captain's cassette on the desk and went up to the surface. It was night and she smoked a cigarette looking towards the other part of the city. It was oddly quiet; as though the war was at last over.

Soon she would go down to her office to transcribe another tape, to write another entry for the book that would be sent to God.

WHITE GOODS

The presentation was coming to an end, or at least Rence hoped it was. He had lost count of the number of slides, fairy dust transitions between each one spraying the screen with sparkles. He hadn't taken in the content except to note the absence of the usual blue and white colour scheme of Task B Industries.

He exhaled and pressed his fingers against his head. He could nod off, he could easily fall asleep but someone was sure to notice. He looked up at the screen for a moment. Another bullet pointed list with words that meant nothing and the presenter, Haynes, his red hair slicked back, compulsively pushing his glasses up his nose bridge and droning on in his nasal voice.

"…and so with Notice we confidently believe we will dominate everything within six weeks of the launch."

Rence swallowed a yawn. There was no way this project, this Notice, was going ahead; this had to be one of the worst presentations he had ever seen.

Then everyone was rising to their feet, clapping and cheering. Next to him some twerp he vaguely recognised as being from Accounts was saying, yes, yes, exhaling as though he was about to come.

Notice was going to be Task B's greatest ever launch. And Rence realised he had no idea at all what it was.

As everyone filed out of the meeting room, back to their offices, he overheard their talking; phrases like 'revolutionary concept' and 'game changing' filled the air. He edged up to one of his colleagues, Colin, who was engrossed in conversation with that Janice from HR. They were smiling as they spoke, nodding. For the first time in weeks everyone had stopped talking about the latest pandemic that had already caused hundreds of deaths in Hungary.

"What do you think?" Colin asked Rence, "so simple isn't it? But then I suppose all the great ideas are."

Rence nodded in time with them, but he must have given something away.

"You don't seem to be too enthusiastic," Janice said loudly. A few heads turned at that, began to look at Rence.

"No, no," Rence held up his hands, "it's brilliant isn't it?"

Back at his computer Rence emailed Haynes immediately.

Wonderful presentation. Could I have a copy of the slides?

The reply came about half an hour later.

Thanks, much appreciated. Slides attached.

But when Rence opened the slides the PowerPoint file consisted of thirty mostly plain white slides; a few had bullet points. Just bullet points without text.

He emailed back.

Some mistake. Wrong presentation?

Rence hadn't even dared to go to the toilet. He could hear people still enthusing about Notice. They were sure to want him to join in. When he finally couldn't hold on any longer he put his head down and fast-walked straight for the door. He made it as far as the small crowd around the photocopier, where Colin appeared in front of him. Rence looked up and saw that almost everyone in the office was standing around talking.

"Need the loo…"

"What's the matter with you?" said Colin, "relax a bit…look, we're all going down the Crown tonight…"

"It's Tuesday."

Rence's bladder really hurt now. He took a few steps towards the door.

"God, Rence," Colin said, "what is the matter with you? Don't you get it?"

"Sure," said Rence, "sure."

And he ran as fast as he could to the door.

Because Colin insisted he went to the pub. The mood was joyous, even ecstatic. Managers were buying enormous rounds of drinks so that everyone was soon tipsy. Rence knew he would have to be careful.

"So what," asked Colin as they stood by the jukebox, "do you make of the implications?"

Rence opened his mouth, trying of think what to say but then the loud-speakers, up on the wall above their heads, mercifully burst into life with loud thrashing guitar music.

"Brilliant," Colin said.

"I mean when Notice is…launched," Rence had to shout.

Colin was nodding in time to the music. "When it goes live? Yeah. Nothing will ever be the same again."

"So we'll corner the market?" Rence said.

"Corner the market!" Was Colin actually pogoing? "You're thinking too small. This is the biggest thing ever."

Then Colin bounced away, into the crowd of Rence's workmates who were already dancing, glasses held high in the air, beer and wine spilling on the floor as the power chords and drumbeat accelerated.

In the morning Rence vowed to forget about Notice, to concentrate on his usual work. He told himself that it was all Emperor's New Clothes. That it would pass. But when he got to work, his usual five minutes early, every desk was occupied. Even the usual slackers were in. Far from being a load of hung-over slatterns they were all banging and clicking away at their computers.

When he passed Colin's desk Colin looked up and shook his head. Rence saw the screen of Colin's PC, saw the blank document, the white screen. All around the office everyone was staring into white screens, blank Word documents that remained blank even as they typed away. By the time he sat down he was sweating. There was an e-mail from Haynes with a cc to Rence's line manager Getch (who was off sick).

You seem to have some hesitation about fully endorsing Notice. Why don't we have a chat in my office? Say 2pm. Nothing formal.

Nothing formal. And yet the cc. It smacked of the usual sort of middle management tactics. But Rence knew there was something different going on here.

There was one other e-mail, from the MD himself and addressed to everyone. Work was to cease on all other projects. All efforts were to go into developing and launching Notice as soon as possible.

But Rence had nothing to do. He had not been given a specific task. He went on the internet where the story had already leaked. Task B Industries. Their product. <u>Innovative</u>. <u>Revolutionary</u>. Columnists were already speculating that it would be bigger than the I-phone, possibly of mobile phones in general. There was general speculation about the role marketing played in modern society and the impacts of innovative design on life.

It was hard to find any other news but scrolling down Rence saw that the pandemic had reached Vienna. Schools were shut and the army had been called out to distribute food to outlying districts. The Swiss were considering closing their borders.

Somewhere, across the office someone sneezed. Rence decided to get on with what he had been doing before: preparing a set of slogans that would later be incorporated into a press release for a new type of drill bit. But when he checked on the shared drive he saw that all his files were gone.

"Hey," he shouted, then looked around. A few people glanced at him but then focused on their screens. He logged a call with IT support and then played Pac-Man on the Arcade Classics site.

Haynes usually slicked back hair was awry, stuck out at angles like odd vegetation. His eyes were red as though he hadn't been sleeping.

"Rence," he said, his voice was loud but he was not shouting, rather it was like he had been turned up a notch. "I've heard you're not really on board with Notice…"

"No…it's….It's not that…"

"Listen, you have to understand how important this is."

Haynes banged his fist down on the desk then looked at it surprised.

"I do…" said Rence, nodding away.

"Do you know," said Haynes, "why there is something rather than nothing?"

Rence tried to think of what to say to this but Haynes was already talking again.

"Perhaps I'm being unfair to you, perhaps we should accept this unevenness, this lack of understanding in some. I think the best thing we can do with you is to start you off on something small, some part of Notice that you might be able to understand. Take this."

He handed Rence a pocket folder.

"Now be off with you."

Back at his desk Rence opened the pocket folder. He expected it to contain blank pages but this was not so. It was a set of designs, drawings and schematics. Then there were some instructions like those for flat-packs from Ikea.

Rectangular boxes. Each with a lid that would hermetically seal and keep the contents fresh. He tried to make sense of the dimensions. Were the units in metres or centimetres? Then he saw the key at the bottom of the page. The units were hand-spans. And there was tiny writing, like the legal conditions on an agreement, a note.

Each corpse will be a slightly different size. It is best to measure before death ideally before the onset of illness. Size may be adjusted with the insertion of section B panels on construction. Additional section B panels may be purchased for your Notice retailer.

These were the manufacturing specifications for Notice. How was this a small part of the project as Haynes had said? Surely it was the most important. But as Rence worked on over the next few weeks, contacting the factories, scanning and sending the specifications, it became clear that what Notice actually was was not at all the most important part of it.

People in the street began to use the word 'Notice' in a different way, with a sort of ironic twist.

Don't you notice how good it is?
Have you noticed?
And they would laugh.
When the launch came it happened simultaneously across the world.

TV ads were mini-epics as popular soap operas were cancelled to screen them. Colin was enthusing about the 'localised global' approach.

"In California they're sold as cryogenic chambers or zero rooms. In India as karmic isolation booths. In China they are gates to the ancestors. The same box becomes the dream of whoever purchases it. Notice is the perfect product."

The news showed footage of airports mobbed as the white boxes were unloaded; shops were overrun. There were riots in queues to purchase Notice. Everyone had to have it. Everyone took Notice.

Over the next few weeks the office, like the streets became emptier as people went off sick. But it was all right because they had their boxes at home.

Colin kept coming in to the last. He collapsed at his desk and one of the remaining security guards hauled him away. He had the privilege of being put in one of the original prototype Notice boxes that had been kept in the basement storage room.

Rence remained in robust health, walking to work because there were no longer any buses, getting askew looks from the few other people around because he didn't wear a facemask. He passed billboard after billboard, white, blank except for the slogan: It's time to give Notice.

The last day he came to work he walked through empty streets. He passed a car that had crashed into the window of a boutique. Tied to the roof was a Notice box, the car driver was dead at the wheel; he hadn't quite made it home.

The office was empty too and Rence wandered through the building going from room to room, turning off computers that had been left on, switching off lights.

In Haynes office he stumbled into the Notice box that was laid on the floor the top sealed. He was about to leave when he heard scratching and a moan from inside.

He took the lid off to find Haynes there, his skin pale and nose running. His eyes, glaucous and magnified through the lenses of his glasses, looked like stranded jellyfish.

"Rence..." Haynes croaked.

Rence had to kneel down to try and catch the words.

"It's been such a tremendous success," Haynes said, "our best launch ever."

Rence waited until Haynes died with a broad smile on his face. Then he put the lid on the box.

After he had turned out the last of the lights in the building he realised that he had never really understood what was going on and that if he tried to turn it into a story it made no sense at all. Better to think of it as a launch, a project and so conclude, as Haynes had done, that it had all been a tremendous success.

CLOWN IN APUS

In the backseat of the Jag, somewhere between Camden Town and Regents Park, Rosco Zen stared at his driver Tunde's head, at the thick shaved neck, as thick as…. What? Thick as Tunde probably. Ha ha. He flicked open his palmtop and extended the no-screen, began to type as it flickered into translucent life projecting a new document unto the back of the driver's chair, the menu options making a band around that thick neck. Perhaps he should write the whole article about Tunde, about how Rosco was allowed a driver because he sometimes got panic attacks on public transport and so had to suffer the ignominy of being bossed around by this comic character.

Probably more interesting than the whole gonzo journo goes to the Zoo bit.

Not that Tunde <u>was</u> thick. Not at all: he could speak three languages and was studying for a PhD in Chinese Economics at SOAS. Driving was just a sideline.

Rosco began to type:

<u>Zoos. With their caged inmates looking like bad cartoon versions of David Attenborough's wet dreams and their guards stomping around with buckets of slops. Did anyone ever really like zoos? But it was all in the name of scientific research they reckoned. Well that's what Doctor Mengele said.</u>

On Parkway there was minor traffic jam. Rosco tapped the palmtop and brought up the bumpf. Background. Crozone Entertainments, new owners of the site. Former headquarters of Zoological Society of London (ZSL). World renowned. Are proud to announce the re-launch…. London privileged to be chosen of host to the sole wormhole portal to the European Organisation for Nuclear Research (CERN) Brane Singularity Chamber (BSC). Blah blah, lots of techno-babble with even more hidden in links for those who loved their science porn hard and explicit. But even Rosco had to admit that creating a universe under tightly controlled laboratory conditions (it kept emphasizing that) was something that might defeat even his hyperbole.

They were on the move again and the Jag made its smooth way around Regents Park to the zoo entrance. There was a large crowd shuffling forward towards the metal revolving doors that had survived the zoo's various reincarnations. There were invited guests, kids who'd won competitions and lots of journalists. Shit. Waiting to enter with all the other journalists was Zoë Scorn.

Tunde parked.

"We're here."

Rosco watched as Zoë chatted and smiled, tossed her shoulder length black hair and made the day of every male around her.

<u>So achingly beautiful it was like being kicked continually in the head just looking at her. Yes, you gazed and were booted over and over again with the pain of knowing you couldn't have her. And you kept on looking.</u>

Rosco had written that about her in his column, <u>Zen Wisdom</u>, once. Not naming her but sometimes he wondered if she knew. If she had always known how he felt since they'd been students together. Perhaps she was secretly laughing at him. He had finished that column with:

<u>I toy with the idea of giving up all worldly pursuits like a latter day anchorite just so I could dedicate all my time to her in excessive devotional masturbation.</u>

"It don't bother me sir, you can sit here all day. But I've got three-thousand words to write on the redevelopment of Shanghai."

"Sure Tunde." Rosco got out of the car.

The press briefing was in a marquee outside the old Elephant House, a giant brutalist edifice like some windowless alien castle of concrete. Rosco remembered it from when he was a kid. He hadn't been back here for decades but since then all the animals had gone. Lots of the mammals slaughtered or shipped out in one of the flu scares. Then in rapid succession it had become <u>London Wildworld</u> (See the lizards and snakes!), <u>London Bugs, Birds and Sealife</u>, <u>London Wings and Fins</u>, and finally <u>Regents Park Aquarium</u>. The fish tanks had survived until a year or two ago, the last remnant of the old ZSL. Each time the place reinvented itself there seemed to be some incident or other. He'd vaguely heard some story about the fish tanks getting smashed. People had began to say the whole site was jinxed.

Zoos. <u>Did anyone ever really like zoos?</u>

Oh yes. Rosco had. He could still recall the wonder of it, the fabulous creatures from picture books suddenly alive, just there beyond the glass or bars. Never the most popular kid he had, for a while, ran with the others on that school visit, entranced as though they had suddenly caught a glimpse down the wardrobe into Narnia.

And then there had been the tiger. Somehow he had got separated from the others, stopped and became entranced. The tiger was a sullen presence within its glassed-in enclosure, pacing with a movement that seemed to ripple the air around it. Till, in response to Rosco tapping the glass it had turned and roared. Rosco had wet himself and had to hold his satchel in front of him all that long hot day as the smell grew worse and worse, becoming a stinking cloud that, to little Rosco, was almost visible.

On the platform the mikes were waiting and a water jug and glasses set out on a table, but the team who were to make the briefing to the press hadn't yet arrived. There seemed to be a genuine buzz of excitement around. He'd passed a clown juggling glittering stars, surrounded by kids, one of whom, a little boy, had a bright tangle of ginger hair. Even the journos were smiling and talking with enthusiasm. He recognised a few of the others, most were proper science correspondents but there were a few culture and entertainment types. Then, approaching him, was the obnoxious rugby-built fart William 'Kensington' Gore of the London <u>Evening News</u>.

"Why on earth did they send you Rosco?" Gore wore a tight white shirt that strained over his huge chest. He looked like an ape at a dress dinner.

"Someone has to make it interesting Bill."

"But there's no showbiz bimbos here, no disgraced game show hosts." His accent was a grating upper-class crowing. "Still if it gets too technical for you just holler."

As he turned and walked away, tossing his abundant blond mane, Rosco gave him a wanker sign.

"Hello Rosco,"

He had smelt her before he registered her presence. Expensive perfume and just beneath it the scents of her body.

"Hello Zoë."

He actually had his eyes closed because he didn't want to look at her. When he did it was like it always was, like looking directly into the sun for a moment, an acute pain followed by an aching afterglow. She looked older, there might have even been a few lines just discernable around her eyes. But like the mole above her lip these just made her a more unique creature.

"You're looking great, as usual," he said, "but I suppose that gets you all the good invitations. So why the fuck are you here, at this thing?"

She sighed, shaking here head. "This is probably the most important scientific experiment ever undertaken. Why are you here?"

"Because this is entertainment. You just wait till the briefing starts. They'll be some slick bod from Crozone with a Disney smile and the gift of eternal youth. Oh they'll let the scruffy scientist talk for five minutes just so we can all pretend. But why do you think they chose this site. It fits perfectly: zoos were always entertainment pretending to be science."

"Do you always have to be so cynical Rosco? I'm sure you weren't like this when we were students."

It was much as Rosco had predicted, a suited youngling from Crozone and a scruffy scientist. Only the scientist was actually a quite pretty young woman whose enthusiasm could have been infectious.

"I had the option of being at the Brane Singularity Chamber, but chose to be here," she gushed, "this is where the action will be. The Wormhole Connectivity Module, the WCM, is actually a particle track that runs around the perimeter of the zoo, the particles there have been entangled with those that will be used to create the singularity. The interface is housed inside the old aquarium, it translates the signals from the WCM into information which we can interpret and graphically represent on the large screens we've got there."

The suit from Crozone coughed.

"Basically," she flustered a bit, "we'll be able to witness the creation of a new universe, the birth of time and space, the separation of the fundamental forces..."

The suit from Crozone stood up at this point and started clapping, managing to get the assembled press to join in and then quieting them with a raised hand and a display of white enamel. He was good. He went on to talk about the state of the art hard-screens and no-screens set up in the aquarium, the triumph of technology the events never seen before that would be witnessed here. The scientist girl looked agitated, kept smiling, then frowning, wondering if she would get another go.

She did. Detailing some of the questions that this experiment might answer, such as were the predictions of string theory correct about the possible existence of ravelled up further dimensions? The possibility of extra dimensions of time as well as space, and those fairly mundane issues like the nature of the initial inflation and further expansion of a universe and what actual shape a it might be. In the end the suit had to shut her up so he could go through the days agenda and let them know where they would get their lunch.

"All the technical details are in the press pack," he said, still smiling, as he waved them out.

The late morning sky had settled into a static uniform grey. Rosco had managed to lose Zoë. He sat on a bench in one of the walkways bordered by flowerbeds and tapped into his palmtop.

I always thought mad scientists were men but not in these enlightened days of equal opportunities.

He looked up when he heard a flapping, wondering for a moment if some of the animals had returned. It was the clown he had seen earlier, his oversized shoes making him walk like a stranded sea bird, lifting each foot slowly making a long stride then flipping it down.

"Hello," he called, he real smile almost wider than his painted one and his stuck-on red nose rising as his own wrinkled beneath it.

Rosco looked around.

No, he is talking to me. I could run for it. He'd never catch me in those shoes.

But the clown was already standing before him.

"You're Rosco Zen aren't you," he said, holding out his hand.

Rosco shook it. "Yes, that's me," he sighed.

"Isn't it great," said the clown, "to be here, today. I mean I just can't believe it. All the kids are great. They're so into it all. Just brilliant the way something like this can get kids into science, isn't it? By the way I'm Oz Cornee."

"Eh?"

"I know what you're thinking: Cornee by name, corny by nature. Ha ha. It's actually my real name, not just my clown name. You were thinking it was my clown name."

"No," said Rosco, "I was thinking that clowns were supposed to be secretly miserable and depressed."

"Not me."

"Shame," Rosco muttered.

But the clown loved Rosco's column, he was a big fan.

"I've got to go," said Rosco, "you know, work."

"Me too," said Oz Cornee, "those kids can be very demanding, but they are great."

At lunch, in the grounds beneath the tiers of the fake cliffs of the Mappin Terrace, Zoë found Rosco and took the seat next to him.

"You always seem to avoid me," she said.

"It's personal," he grinned.

"We used to be friends."

Rosco ignored this and noisily dismembered a prawn. "You still with that hack at the FT?"

"Simon's hardly a hack. He's the deputy international editor. He's written several books on world trade. And he's just had a novel published."

Rosco tried extracting the last bits of meat from the prawn's tail with his tongue and his teeth. "A novel. Jesus."

"You wrote a novel."

Rosco held his arms out as though to be cuffed. "It's a fair cop but please be lenient your honour. It was only attempted literature not pre-meditated middlebrow. For which," he raised a finger to make his point, "they should bring back hanging."

"Actually," Zoë took a sip from her wine, "I liked your novel."

Rosco reached for another prawn.

"Rosco," she said, "are you so scared of being accused of pretension that you can't be genuine at all anymore?"

"Come on Zoë," he spoke with his mouth half full, "we both know that novel writing is just externalized mental illness. I mean," he thought for a moment, "perhaps all writing is that--not what the shrinks say, wanking in public or flashing your tits for the boys--no just a long slow breakdown."

"I thought you wrote because you had something to say to your loyal readership."

"Don't even start me on readers. I just met one and he was a fucking clown. Literally."

After that they didn't talk much. It was a long time till they were due at the big switch on and all the while it was, as he had once written, like being kicked in the head, over and over.

The entrance to the aquarium was narrow and a queue had formed. Rosco managed to jostle his way to the back losing Zoë in the process, coming dangerously close to William Gore but then secreting himself with some weirdoes from obscure physics journals. As he shuffled forward like an animated corpse, he saw the clown, Oz Cornee, standing by himself by the edge of another of those flowerbeds. He beckoned to Rosco. He kept it up till Rosco could no longer pretend he hadn't seen.

"What?" Rosco demanded.

The clown had become remarkably dishevelled since earlier, like flowers that needed throwing out. His greasepaint smile had smudged into a red smear across one cheek, his face looked lined and his eyes rimmed. Rosco noticed that he was now wearing trainers instead of the long clown shoes.

"There's going to be an accident Rosco," he said.

There was no longer the manic grin but the clown managed a wistful smile.

"What are you talking about?" Rosco said.

"Don't worry. You'll survive."

"Look," Rosco concluded the man was obviously deranged, "I've got to get a decent view." He pointed towards the aquarium.

"Goodbye," the clown said.

Rosco turned and saw the last of the queue enter. When he turned back the clown had gone. It was a neat trick; Rosco hadn't heard him move or seen anything.

Inside there were no chairs but a polite crowd packed into the long narrow gallery that was lined with irregular oblong gaps where the fish tanks had once been. Further along the walls were covered with hard screens and above, at intervals were no-screen projections. At the far end of the gallery was the control centre of the experiment, housed inside a container module. It was like a mobile home fitted with large plate glass windows so that those outside could see the scientists work at their terminals, which were chunky and old-fashioned. From here they would control the feed to the screens from the wormhole that was in turn connected with the Brane Singularity Chamber where the new universe would be born. The feed would be broadcast to the rest of the world but there was, Rosco had to admit, something about being here even as he tried to tell himself that he could have stayed at home and sat in his dressing gown drinking tea and watching it all on TV.

He stayed at the edge of the crowd with a good view of the control centre and one of the screens.

"You've found a good spot then," Zoë said, "I knew you would."

"Yes," he said, not looking at her, "but the closer we get to the blast off the more the utter pointlessness of this exercise threatens to overwhelm me."

"Rosco this is, this is… big science."

"I love science. I've got a toilet seat with runway lights so I can piss in the dark, that's science."

"Why do you have to pretend to be such a philistine? Even you can't be unimpressed by the creation of a universe."

Suddenly Rosco saw Oz Cornee flapping towards him from the middle of the crowd, people making way for him. His make-up was fresh as it had been in the morning and he had his clown shoes on again. He waved at Rosco, then held up his finger to indicate he'd be over in a minute. Then from a shoulder bag he took out a pair of trainers, knelt down and took of his clown shoes, put the trainers on lacing them up tightly.

"That man," said Rosco, "is a fucking lunatic."

"Mr Zen, Rosco," the clown held out his hand again, took Rosco's and shook it, "isn't this so exciting."

Rosco introduced Zoë. Why should he suffer alone?

"That was very clever what you did outside," said Rosco, "the vanishing act."

The clown frowned for a second, "Sorry?"

"Just now. When you said something about an accident. Obviously you aren't too worried about it."

"What do you mean accident?" The frown returned.

"Just now. Outside."

"You haven't been smoking that wacky baccy have you Rosco?" the clown laughed nervously.

"Could there be an accident?" Zoë asked.

"Well," Oz Cornee thought for a moment, "there's all sorts of possibilities. Creation of a black hole that could eat the Earth is the one people usually talk about. Of course if somehow the singularity explosion leaked into our universe it could have catastrophic effects. Some people think it could even alter the basic parameters of physics. Not only would life be impossible but even basic chemistry couldn't happen. Someone on the internet even thought that the new universe might somehow form as a bubble inside our own, displacing ours."

"Is any of this likely?" Zoë asked.

"No, no. The new universe will be totally sealed off from ours, creating its own space and time. Well so they say but…"

"Jesus," said Rosco, "what do you know you're a clown?"

"Actually," said he said, "I've got a degree in physics."

"You've got a degree in physics?"

"Yes. I asked especially to come along to this job. Pestered the lady at the agency till she gave in."

"You've got a degree in physics. Then why are you a clown?"

"I like being a clown."

And finally after some minutes of absence Oz Cornee's grin returned.

Ladies and Gentlemen, said the intercom in a voice so bland it was hard to tell what sex it was or what continent it had originated on, the greatest experiment in the history of the human race is about to begin.

The screens kept flashing between different, helpfully labelled shots. There was the exterior of the BSC which looked to Rosco like the business end of ancient steam engine boiler with dials and portholes, only much larger as shown from the people walking on gantries fixed to its front. Then they went to the WCM, the great sewage pipe that ran around the perimeter of the zoo. Then it was down the wormhole to inside the BSC itself, which was just a blacked out screen.

Zoë whispered: "And the Earth was without form, and void; and darkness was upon the face of the deep. And the Spirit of God moved upon the face of the waters."

Rosco could see her intent on the screens, and Oz Cornee was enraptured. But Rosco felt a familiar fluttering at the top of his stomach and an increase in his heart rate. It was the onset of one of the panic attacks he could get on crowded trains or buses. Now though it was because of the clown.

"Zoë," Rosco said, "we've got to get out of here."

"Don't be silly Rosco, we'll miss…"

"What if he's right? What if there's going to be some sort of accident."

The clown must have heard. "You wouldn't be able to outrun it. It won't matter where you are."

But as it turned out the clown was entirely wrong about that.

The parameters for the new universe have been set, said the sexless, placeless voice. But it was suddenly cut off.

"Everyone," said a Geordie accent, and Rosco could see it was one of the scientists inside the command centre holding a wireless mike, "needs to evacuate this building as quickly as possible, there's a problem with the feedback into the interface."

Someone cut in saying something about not needing to go into the details. Then there was a rush for the doors. Rosco clung to Zoë's hand and was pushed forward. Above the agitation of the crowd, voices beginning to have the edge of panic, he heard a familiar intonation, ordering people to make way for a pregnant woman. Across the way, blond hair shaking as he dispensed his commands, William 'Kensington' Gore was keeping his head, slowly shepherding everyone around him to safety.

Rosco had lost sight of Oz Cornee but it turned out the clown had hung back, a real hero, he'd seen an elderly journalist fall and hit his head. After the aquarium was clear of all the spectators the clown appeared at the door holding the famous old Fleet Street soak over his shoulders in a fireman's lift. There was a half-ironic cheer from the journalists who'd begun to regroup outside, urged by their instinctive professional curiosity.

Oz Cornee laid his burden down. He stretched his arms out and was about to say something. Rosco, who'd been recovering his breath by sitting on the floor, stood up and came forward to greet him. Rosco noticed that the clown's smile had smudged into a red smear over one cheek. Then there was a flash of light and a shockwave that threw Rosco and many others to the ground. Oz Cornee vanished.

For a moment Rosco thought that he'd pissed himself, he felt wet seeping up the seat of his trousers and onto his legs. Then he noticed that there was water coming from the open doors of the aquarium.

"What's going on?" Zoë asked, helping Rosco up.

On one of the steps to the aquarium there was something moving, flashing lemon and maroon, flapping in the growing stream of water.

"It's a fish," Rosco said.

He saw others now, the rainbow colours of warm waters and the dull gunmetal of colder seas. The water was coming faster, pouring out the doors and making the steps into a cataract. There were fish and various other sea creatures struggling and flipping, some managing to swim as the water rose.

"But there weren't any fish in there," someone said.

For a moment the flow from the door seemed to abate, becoming a trickle, but Rosco saw that it hadn't stopped. Something was caught in the door, like a giant slab of breathing granite, which eventually struggled free, rolled down the steps and gasped in water too shallow for it to breath. Even as it died the shark made a malevolent presence.

Already cameras were in action capturing what they thought would be the picture of the year.

"Come on," said Rosco said to Zoë, "my driver's waiting outside. Let's leave this to the corpsedogs."

"That poor man," she said.

"Well," said Rosco, "he's sure going to get a good write-up laying down his life for a hack in front of a horde of other hacks."

They made their way to the main zoo exit and Rosco followed Zoë through the revolving doors, then wondered if they'd come the right way. This wasn't the road where Tunde was parked in the Jag. It seemed they had come into another part of the zoo; there were the familiar paths and benches and the empty enclosures. But Rosco could also see the Mappin Terrace, the Elephant House.

"But we've just come from over there. How come we have got around the back of it?" Zoë asked.

Rosco didn't want to think about this. "Come on."

He turned to lead Zoë back through the revolving doors except they weren't there. They were inside the high fence and hedges that ran around the zoo perimeter. Trying to laugh he said, "How'd we get out of this place?"

Just then a crowd walked through the fence.

"What?" said a bewildered man as he pulled his teenage daughter through behind him.

Over the next few hours every attempt to leave the zoo failed. The revolving doors of the main entrance led to the same spot that Zoë and Rosco had found which was, according to an old fold out guide that Rosco had found, the camel house on the opposite side of the zoo. It wasn't difficult to try other routes because the high fencing had changed so that when someone tried to climb it they had just fallen through finding themselves somewhere else in the zoo. Even when you looked out the view was no longer of the park or the surrounding streets but of zoo buildings, the roof of the Elephant House, the high bars of aviaries. The afternoon seemed interminable, the same slate grey sky above without alteration in the light.

Soon, many had given up trying to leave. Most had congregated in or around in Barclay Court where the restaurant, souvenir shop and porters lodge was located. There was food here, laid out for an evening reception. Not to mention a stock room full of booze.

Rosco had sat outside on a bench for a while listening while the journos took centre stage predicting the rescue attempt that would be going on. Then the boffins from the science magazines would start speculating. He could see through the window of the restaurant where William Gore was telling people how they should be distributing the food. When Rosco was sure Zoë was immersed in some discussion about what had possibly happened--which he assumed was basically bullshit because how could anyone know--he took off to explore.

The area around the aquarium was empty now, not only of people but also of the fish and any remnants of them. There wasn't even a smell. It was only when Rosco focused his attention on the sky, noticing that evening still hadn't arrived, that from the corner of his eye he glimpsed a great stain of water scattered with the dead creatures he had seen before, including the vast solidity of the shark. Inside, the aquarium was now lit only by the faint glow from the open door behind him so that shadow had crept into every corner. There was the long cavernous gallery, the bare sockets where the fish tanks had once been and further on the hard-screens. But alongside this Rosco glimpsed, he could say no more than that, the cracked and broken lines of the tanks. Then, for a brief moment, Rosco saw people. They walked, pausing before the tanks, moving slowly as though underwater.

When he called out he was sure a woman who had been peering into one of the tanks turned, just for a second. But then she was gone entirely.

Further in he at last approached the command centre, but even in the gloom he could see there was no hope of learning anything here. It was blown to pieces.

On his way back out he saw people again. They were like reflections seen in glass, barely there at all really, the colours bled from their clothes and skin. Then, standing among the crowd of these ghosts, but solid, real and technicolour, Rosco saw Oz Cornee, juggling stars. The clown saw him, waved, and let a star fall. Then he disappeared along with his spectral audience.

Outside Rosco wandered. Past ice-cream booths and abandoned cages, some not much bigger than chicken runs others, like one with a rope and tire swing, vast baroque complexes with open spaces and scaffolding, adjoining rooms and passages. There always seemed to be more of everything than he remembered, more cages, more aviaries, little corners with benches, toilet blocks, mini-amphitheatres and strange art-deco penguin pools.

He came to the foot tunnel that led to the part of the zoo located to the north of the Regents Park ring road. He guessed that if he followed it he would just loop around and enter the zoo somewhere else. The boundary of their confinement, he assumed, was the path the Wormhole Connectivity Module had traced around the main zoo area. Just inside the tunnel entrance though he could see the murals reproducing the Lascaux cave paintings where a solitary fallen hunter lay amidst endless godlike beasts. Here was one of humanity's first efforts to depict the world, not just the beginning of art but of science too.

Should have guessed the mad scientists would get us in the end.

But it wasn't funny.

He activated his palmtop and wrote that same sentence down. Felt better.

As he turned to make his way back to the restaurant he noted that it still wasn't getting any darker. The sky hadn't changed and he wandered through this elongated afternoon with the short walk seeming to take hours even though the clock on his palmtop told him otherwise. It was as if the minutes were stretched out like a corridor that suddenly reaches endlessly before you in a dream.

He'd never had one of those dreams but had seen plenty of films.

Barclay Court had the atmosphere of a faux night with fires burning in litter bins under the unchanging afternoon sky, and music coming from some portable device, a heavy rhythmic beat that repeated its signature with only minor variations. In the space between the fires people were dancing, clutching wine bottles. To one side William Gore sat in a deck chair watching, not drinking, focused on a young woman who was dancing alone totally caught in the rhythm. She had stripped down to a plain black bra.

It was Zoë.

"Good to have you back Rosco," someone (not her) called out drunkenly.

"Come on."

"We could all be dead by tomorrow."

Rosco scampered away to find somewhere to sleep.

When he woke Rosco headed back to the restaurant to try and get some kind of breakfast. He saw Zoë coming from the toilets her face glistening wet from washing. He had seen her like this once before--when she'd emerged from the room of one of his flatmates at university—without makeup, hair a mess that she'd swept behind her ears. Astonishingly and artlessly beautiful.

"I've been looking for you," she said, "where have you been?"

"What is this, you're not my mum. And anyway I'm sure you found someone."

He still had the image of her dancing, almost undressed, while 'Kensington' fucking Gore ogled.

"My God Rosco, what is on your mind? This is possibly the end of the world and you just carry on taking cheap shots."

"Last time I saw you looked like you were at a rave."

"People needed to let off a little steam. Even Bill saw that…"

" 'Bill' now is it?"

"Rosco it's been bordering on the terrifying the last few days. There are kids crying, there were grown men crying. The bloody science hacks don't help talking about never being able to communicate with outside. Bill ordered them to be on their palmtops just in case there is contact. Even the mobile phones have gone weird; they don't work more than a few metres away from each other. There's some sort of time delay."

But Rosco didn't understand.

"What do you mean 'the last few days'? We've only been here since yesterday."

"Look, I know it's difficult to reckon because it never gets dark but we must have been here the best part of a week. And while you've been off doing whatever people are trying to get organised. So don't just wander into the kitchen and grab what you like. There's a food distribution system now. Bill reckons we've got enough to last for about a month."

"Oh," Rosco blew out a sarcastic laugh, "Kensington's in charge is he? Are you playing Tarzan and he Jane?"

She held her hands to her temples.

"Rosco will you stop it? This isn't the time or place for this. But for the record I like you. I've always liked you but you never made a move when you should have did you? All you did was make clever little quips."

No, he'd never made a move. Even the night they'd spent together after their finals, drinking Guinness and talking about every thing they were going to do with their lives. When the dawn came he still had not dared come any closer, still had not touched her. Then it was too late.

It would have been like grabbing the blades of chainsaw.

Except that it wouldn't.

From the restaurant a line of men emerged carrying boxes and table. Gore was there, not carrying anything, just pointing, ordering. Then he saw Rosco and Zoë and came over.

"So your back Rosco. Just like your sort to go fucking AWOL when there's crisis."

"It was one night," Rosco murmured.

"Shut up you shit."

What was it about posh people swearing? It sounded like they were speaking a foreign language, badly.

Gore turned to Zoë, reached out to try and touch her elbow, which she just moved away in time.

"Zoë, my dear," he said, "will you come over and help pass out some of the rations?"

Rosco found the nearest bench and flicked on his no-screen and began to type into his palmtop.

Suddenly Gore was looming over him. "What are you doing? You should be helping" he almost spat.

"I'm getting on with my job. Writing the story."

"Don't you get it? There's no-one to read your drivel now. I've had people scanning every possible wavelength for communication. They think that we're all that's left. If you transmitted your precious story it would just bounce around the zoo till the signal decayed. What's the point?"

"Well," Rosco shrugged, "if this really is the end it's one story that I wouldn't want to miss."

"There's a good chance we could all die here, even if we do pull together."

"I could have died on the way here. I mean a lorry could have crashed into my car. Or I could've had a heart attack wanking in the bath, or…"

But Rosco knew it was bravado. He felt strangely calm about the situation but not, as he made out, because he didn't care. There was something about the zoo, something he had to understand.

"Almost everyone," Gore was saying, "that you've ever known is dead. Don't you get it? I had a wife. I had two sons. They're dead."

For a moment he caught a flicker of something human in the mass of rugby flesh and Oxbridge confidence. Then Rosco thought of the people he'd known. His parents were long dead. He tried to think of ex-girlfriends but found himself thinking about Tunde, his driver, about all the places they'd been around London, of Tunde's family in Nigeria connected by thoughts and phones and money cables; of Tunde's mind ranging across the complexities of the Chinese economy, the millions of people, their buying habits, their contribution to Gross National Product. All gone.

He saw Zoë handing out snack bars to a woman with a child. It was the little boy with the bright ginger hair.

"I've got to get out of here," he said, standing.

"Coward."

Near to a line of identical small cages he found a kiosk and raided it for chocolate, crisps, cartons of juice. Then lit off away from Barclay Court and the restaurant. He consulted his zoo guide. What should have been the ten-minute saunter to the old lion enclosure took most of what he thought of as that morning. There seemed to be more and more of the same structures: paths, cages, toilets, information booths, kiosks and lodges. It was impossible to track the passage of time with the unchanging light. The palmtop told him eight minutes and thirty-three seconds had passed but he was already hungry again. Perhaps that was the only thing he could trust, the internal progression of his body, the metabolic process that managed his own change and slow decay.

The lion enclosure was a fake veldt surrounded by bars, a fence and a moat. He remembered it vaguely from his childhood visit, but not because of the lions which had been distant and aloof. He remembered it because near here was the tiger.

Just as he was tucking into his third chocolate bar he heard the sound, which at first he thought might be the squeaking of an un-oiled wheel. Then he realised what it was and began to jog towards the giant aviaries he could see in the distance. When he eventually reached them he stopped panting. At ground level the aviaries were just like the other cages, overgrown with weeds and rotten food and droppings. But when he looked up he was overcome by their majesty. These were largest cages of all, great cathedrals of steel lattice capturing quadrants of sky.

There was no trace of the sound that had brought him here, only a slight breeze through the jumble of planted reeds. Then, as though appearing from an unseen slit in the air, dropping like a dead weight, a bird appeared, some nameless tropical dandy with a copper wings and egg-yolk head, that fell for a few feet calling out with a joyous scream. It was quickly joined by others of its species, then more varied companions similarly extravagant, all falling from nowhere, till in unison the whole flock began to beat their wings flying up again in an arc. As he traced their path to the far side of the aviary they all funnelled together and vanished into another unseen rip in the air.

Then it happened again: the drop from their point of origin, rising in flight and then disappearance. And again, so that Rosco felt caught in a rhythm of empty silent sky then flashes of colour and song. He didn't know how long he'd been watching when someone next to him spoke.

"Beautiful aren't they. Birds of Paradise. Apus."

For a moment he didn't recognise the speaker who was dressed in raw animal skins. The face was familiar but there was something different. No make-up.

"Oz Cornee?"

"Good to see you again," the clown said. With his face naked he looked older, the lines from his eyes spreading back to give him a wrinkled, weathered appearance.

"I thought you were dead but then you I saw you. I saw things, visions. I don't know," Rosco knew he wasn't making sense. "What's going on?"

Oz pointed up at the birds.

"They're following a different arrow of time. Like the light of starts they've come out of the past, to now. I expect that's where they disappear to. Round and round. The expansion must have reached the era when the aviary was stocked. Expect surprises Rosco."

"But how are you here?"

The clown shrugged. "I was caught in the heart of it. At the beginning of a new universe with its dimensions of time and space unravelling."

"What do you mean?"

"Look," Oz pointed to the aviary again, "I think they've finally left us."

Rosco realised that the silence had returned, looked into the aviary, at its vast expanse enclosing nothingness. Then, like his aquarium vision, the aviary was suddenly filled, the reeds tall and proud, the birds on perches and flitting from here to there. Then all that was gone again.

"What's going on?" he asked.
But the clown had gone too.

He couldn't tell how long it took to get back to Barclay Court and the settlement around the restaurant. It was easy to get lost now, even walking in a straight line seemed to take him past duplicates of the same building. When he saw anything that looked like it might contain birdlife he kept clear still hearing the occasional beat of wings or call. Eventually he thought he recognised a particular cage, a certain kiosk. When he stumbled to the edge of Barclay Court it was meal-time again. Zoë was there with some of the other women doling out food. She looked tired and dishevelled. Near the restaurant he saw Gore, pointing, directing. When Gore saw Rosco he marched over.

"Just like you to run out as we're getting organised. Where have you been all this time?"

"I'm tired," Rosco said.

"Sleep then. We'll sort you out some jobs when you wake up."

Rosco wandered into the restaurant which had been turned into a dormitory. Here people lay on beds made from drapes, table clothes and sacking. On one of these, sitting up at a no-screen he recognised one of the science journalists. Around another a woman huddled a child in her lap. All Rosco could see of the child was the mass of bright ginger hair.

Rosco knew there was no way he could stay here. Back outside he approached the old souvenir shop thinking he might find refuge there, but the door was padlocked.

"That's the store room now," Zoë said.

She wiped her hands on the front of her dirty trousers.

"Oh," was all Rosco could think of to say.

"William organised it all."

" 'William' is it now."

"Look," she touched Rosco's arm, "I know he can be uptight but he pulled it together. He just got on with things. You don't know what it was like here."

"I've not been far, I..." But he couldn't begin to explain. The birds. Oz Cornee.

Zoë looked ground down, nearly beaten.

"I need to get some sleep," he said and walked away to a nearby path and lay down on a bench there.

When he woke he could voices in Barclay Court and he wandered up the path only to meet a journo he vaguely recognised holding some kind of rifle.

"Shit Rosco," he said, "what are you doing?"

"What are *you* fucking doing?"

"Keeping guard. William told us to..."

"Fuck William. And where'd you get that gun?"

"William found it. In the lodge with all the vet supplies."

Rosco stood for a minute. He could see into Barclay Court a woman emptying a bucket. Presumably the slops from the night. He turned and walked in the other direction.

"Where you going?" the guard asked.

"Away from here," Rosco called back.

Away. Not bothering to try and keep track of where he was heading. Soon though he found a bench and started up his palmtop, filled with the need to make sense of it all.
Jesus was wrong, he typed and set this as a cross-head.
When it comes to inheriting the Earth the meek didn't get a look in. Did you ever think they would? No, new head boy and prefect is none other than rugby fetishist and deranged Sloane, William Kensington Gore. The word 'meek' would only figure in his vocabulary as the sound some hunted creature might make just before it was about to be savaged by dogs or bazookered by a bunch of braying toffs. Meek, meek, meek. Billy it seems has set himself up as generalissimo of this banana republic. It's one ape one vote and Bill is that ape.

He formatted the file, then for some reason hit the transmit button that would normally send the story directly to the editorial desk. Maybe it would journey into whatever passed for outer space here, bits of encoded information travelling for billions of years looking for an audience.

Over the next few days, as far as he could measure them in this eternal afternoon, he moved towards what he hoped was the edge of the zoo but never to reached it. He raided kiosks, that always were miraculously supplied with goodies, although the particular type changed, chocolate bars and brands of crisps he remembered from when he was a kid began to be appear. He made sure that everyday he sat down to write something. Usually about Gore, whose organisational zeal Rosco built into a conceit about political ambition, the arrogance of the English upper-classes, public school over-confidence in the face of armageddon, the pointlessness of liking rugby and hunting and polo, and the man's posh accent and general tosserness. Rosco always transmitted his reports, wondering at the confusion they would cause the alien race that might one day read them. It kept him occupied as he tried not to pay too much attention to the life that was stirring all around him, the scatterings behind glass, the howls of monkeys, the roars and hoots.

Rosco got lost. He grew frightened by the glimpses he caught, of zebras, bison and monkeys. Sometimes when ghostly crowds of people wandered past he felt their wake softly against his skin. He came to an enclosure of solid plate glass, an overgrown landscape inside with a dried out pool.

He remembered this place.

Inside he watched the air disturbed, like heat over tarmac, a wave of orange and black. After it had gone—like thunder following light—a roar came, a wave of sound that he convinced himself he could feel, even as he ran away.

Fucking tiger.

He wanted to laugh and joke, indulge in some kind of routine about running so fast it was like Road Runner, meep, meep. But the primeval terror that filled him tore away any ability to mock.

Get back then. Get back to where the others were even if it meant enduring Gore and his tin-pot dictatorship. Only Rosco didn't know which way to go. The zoo had magnified, extended. As he wandered on there were more apparitions, of people, of animals of every kind, no longer confined to cages or enclosures. Then, at last, there was something real. Lying on the path before him was the body of a large grazing mammal. It was difficult to tell what it was since it had been ripped and large parts of it eaten. Some sort of deer perhaps, hunted and killed.

Rosco didn't stop after that till he found somewhere he recognised, a kiosk snack bar he had been to before. Outside on one of the tables were wrappers he had left. The endless afternoon was filled with the sounds of animals, the cries and barks, the calls of birds that he sometimes thought he could hear whizzing directly overhead. At one point, barricaded inside the kiosk, a chair against the door, he heard the roar again. Even in the distance its impact shook him and for a few moments the other sounds fell into silence. When at last the other creatures resumed their clamour they seemed cowed and timid.

He didn't sleep much in the kiosk. When he half drifted absurd plans formed. Hansel and Gretel stone dropping or pulling apart his jumper to make a Theseus thread. At least that way he could avoid continually doubling back. But when he woke up he was no longer even sure that he'd been to this particular kiosk before. Perhaps the wrappers had been left by someone else.

He walked on, trying to ignore the ghostly visitors in family packs and shapes of animals all around. Then, once more, he came across something tangible. Another mauled body but now the species was clearly recognisable. The woman's legs, almost severed around the thighs, were in what appeared to be woollen stockings. On here head —largely untouched—was the sort of bonnet that had been fashionable when Winston Churchill was still in the wilderness.

Rosco closed her eyes, took what remained of her cardigan and covered her face then walked away and sat down. Still shaking he turned on his palmtop and typed out a report, as factual as possible, of what he had seen. Then:

<u>Perhaps this is the final irony. At the end of it all the animals are getting their revenge. Right here, where we kept them prisoners.</u>

When he continued on his journey now it was with slow steps. Instead of trying to ignore what he could no longer dismiss as mere visions, he looked closely. There were people laughing, pointing at the wonders. Sometimes the animals were in the same locale as these people, happily caged and on display. Other times it was as though they were somewhere else, like the pack of wolves that ran along a footpath, straight through a group of oblivious visitors. Occasionally someone would notice Rosco, smile or frown at him, but most of the time he passed among them as though he were floating underwater among translucent jellyfish who hardly had the organs to detect he existed at all. There was a kind of intoxication about this wanderings, a revelling in this effloresce of life that made Rosco the ghost, the creature from the afterlife.

He was in this state of blissful immersion when he wandered into a little clearing centred around an ornamental fountain. Next to the fountain stood a man, his once rugged looks somehow aged into grey fatigue. His clothes had been repaired many times. It was moment before Rosco realised that it was William Kensington Gore. He was holding a rifle.

When he saw Rosco he starred at him. He hadn't yet raised the gun.

Gore gave a long sigh, "Not writing Rosco? Not scribbling away your clever little remarks."

"Bill," Rosco began, his momentary relief at being found already gone.

"It got through you see," said Gore, "undermined my authority."

Rosco had no idea what he was talking about.

"Bill, I've been lost. There's animals... people."

Gore suddenly raised the rifle, pointed it for a moment then rested it over his shoulder. He wasn't listening to Rosco at all.

"There was a group of boffins," Gore said, "from the science magazines. Sat at their no-screens trying to pick up signals from outside. They kept saying there was no way any signals could get through. One of them even said there was no 'outside' anymore. I made him shut up. Didn't want to frighten people. I made them keep at it, keep scanning for communication. People need hope. It's part of what could help us survive. Then, I'd see them at their screens giggling. Calling others over."

"Oh."

"You know how difficult it's been to try and maintain some order? To try and plan some kind of life for us all here? It's relied on strong leadership and you undermined it. You couldn't cope with any responsibility yourself so you had to have a dig at me."

"They picked up my reports."

"Yes."

"Look, Bill..."

"All those clever little skits on me being a toff, the gibes about rugby. I don't even like rugby you know that? But you were right about one thing though. I do like hunting. I'll hold my hand up to that." He smiled. "Except I can't hold up my hand seeing as I'm carrying this rifle. You see Rosco I hunted you. Tracked you like a beast. Followed your trail of sweet wrappers and crisp packets. You would leave garbage behind you. You've been doing it your whole career."

At last he levelled the rifle.

"Bill..."

"She asked me to come and look for you. Bring you back but you've been gone so long chances are I never found you. No one else will ever come. It's too far now. Or," Gore suddenly had an idea, "I did find you, all chewed up by some animal."

Rosco lifted his hand to his face as though to stop the bullet, but even as Gore shifted his weight, sighted down the barrel, a blur of frenzied motion slashed through the air.

The tiger was beneath Gore's guard before he could react, claws first it threw its whole weight against him, knocking him to the ground. Gore tried to swing the rifle to strike a blow even as he fell but his grip failed as the tiger ripped into his chest. The gun clattered to the ground.

"Kill..." Gore managed to say before his voice was mangled into a scream, yet all the while he was trying to punch and kick, his blows showing a ferocity almost matching that of the tiger.

Rosco ran over and picked up the rifle, then ran down the track, needing to be away from the screaming. When he turned and looked back into the clearing the tiger was still at his work. Gore would already be dead, but what if the tiger came after him? He walked forward slowly, trying to aim as the rifle shook in his hands.

Then, as he took another step closer, the tiger stopped its chewing and looked up at him, for a moment absolutely still, its presence like a weight in the air.

I will do this, Rosco told himself.

The tiger roared, the force of it making Rosco quiver. He felt pressure in his bladder.

When Rosco pulled the trigger the bullet threw up dust far behind the fountain. The tiger began to move in elegant silence towards him, its eyes fixing Rosco to the spot. The instant the tiger leapt Rosco knew he had no chance, now way to outrun it. He pulled the trigger again but nothing happened. He didn't really know what he was doing.

This is it then.

He watched the path of the animal's leap, watched it in mid-air disappear into nothingness.

It was sometime, possibly days, later before he could write about what had happened. Under the title 'Obituary' he wrote a matter-of-fact account. Then:

<u>I could never pretend to like him. The man was an arse of the first order and I could wax ironic about his death: the hunter becoming the hunted. Blah blah. In the end I'd just like to set the record straight.</u>
<u>1. I believe he would have shot me.</u>
<u>2. He died fighting.</u>
<u>3. He was, after all, not particularly fond of rugby.</u>

The journey back must have taken weeks. There was always food to be found, stranger and more archaic tit bits from kiosks that themselves appeared increasingly to have the trappings of bygone ages, pasted adverts for attractions in pastel colours, prices in old money. He learnt to use the rifle and brought down a deer, cooked it and lived off it for a time. All the while he moved through the half-life of old visitors, old animals that sometimes became real. More and more Rosco resembled an old tramp which made the respectable Edwardian families keep their distance on the occasions when they saw him.

Somewhere half-familiar, with the fake cliffs of the Mappin Terrace or some version of it, spreading across the horizon, he met Oz Cornee for the last time.

"Hello Rosco," the clown greeted him, bright and cheerful, but without make-up, his face aged.

"I'm trying to find my way back," said Rosco, "find Zoë and the others. Perhaps we <u>can</u> start again. Perhaps there is a chance."

He had been thinking about his a lot. Somehow there no longer seemed anything to fear. She would be waiting and he would be there for her. It might not, after all, be too late.

"Oh yes," said Oz, "there's always a chance. It's taken you a long time though Rosco hasn't it."

"What's happened here Oz? What went wrong when they turned the machine on?"

The clown shrugged. "I'm not sure anything went wrong. Not really. They wanted to create a new universe and they have. That universe has taken what it found here as its raw materials, so it's a universe populated not with stars and galaxies but with the zoo and everything that's ever been here. Like the old universe this one has inflated, expanded, stretched further and further, not only in space but in time as well. If you've been travelling with it Rosco then you've been going very fast, travelling a long way. I think it's time you got back."

And before he vanished he told Rosco to keep heading for the Mappin Terrace mountain range.

As he came near he smelt smoke, carrying the odour of burnt fat so strongly he could feel it stick to his tongue and his teeth. He came into Barclay Court and could see that the whole area had changed. The restaurant and the other buildings looked as though they had decayed, the brickwork weathered and overgrown with ivy. To Rosco it looked like some bizarre film set, people in animal skins going about primitive activities, slicing at carcasses that roasted over an open fire, scraping animal hides.

Like something out of a bad jungle take-off from a sketch show, an almost giant of a man walked towards him carrying a spear, dressed in rawhide. The man's hair was a tangle of bright ginger. Behind him an old woman hobbled forward. There was something familiar about her, as though the cracked and worn skin of her face, the mole above her lip, were a mask he could see beneath.

"Is Zoë here?" Rosco managed to say.

But before the old woman even spoke Rosco already knew.

DAWN IN THE GARDEN OF ENGLAND

In his castle Edwin Mourne, the Dryhten of Kent, stood at the mirror admiring himself in his underwear. Behind him his butler Rigby held two jackets, one a long-tailed black affair the other a dress tunic with epaulettes ingeniously fashioned in the sun rune of the New Dawn. Without turning the Dryhten drew in a breath before intoning, "<u>Ich the vader of oure Cantware, y-wyte hou it y-event thet this is seide mid Engliss of Kent.</u>"

"Well?" said the Dryhten when Rigby still hadn't responded.

"Sir?"

"Boffins at Canterbury. It's in Kentish. They say that soon we'll be able to issue interfaces to a language acquisition application. Within half a generation we'll be speaking the genuine ancestral tongue. As it was before being diluted by Norman French. What do you think?"

"I think the tunic sir. It carries more of an air of authority."

"Must you insist on playing Jeeves?"

"More of a Lear's fool, sir."

"I don't know why I tolerate you Rigby. Perhaps because I must tolerate someone. If I disposed of everyone who displeased me I would be little more than a monster."

"As you will sir. Have you decided on your apparel for this evening?"

"Leave them both. I'll choose soon enough. You can go now."

When he was alone the Dryhten sat at his desk. Beside the antique fountain pen and sheaf of writing paper was the palimpsest of reports he had already gone over with Rigby. The forestation was proceeding apace and the relocation of the non-Kentish population to the slums of south-east London would soon be complete. All was in place for the celebration of the twentieth anniversary of the New Dawn. There was just one check he wanted to make and he had to be on his own for that. Even Rigby knew nothing about Project Bestiary.

He rolled up his sleeve and from the drawers of the desk pulled out an interface, a green blob that began to melt into a gel as soon as he had poured it onto his skin. He could still feel himself in the seat in his dressing room, the weight of his body in the old chair. He was even able to fade in his vision so that he came back entirely. Now though he let himself be totally immersed into the viewpoint of Crawley, the Project Thane, who stood on the edge of a forest clearing. Crawley gave him another tedious explanation of the conversion process from the raw material to the final outcome. But the Dryhten cut him off. Apart from being slightly squeamish he wasn't interested in the details. Leave that to the likes of Crawley. The Dryhten liked instead to contemplate the final seasoning he was adding to the spell he had been so long brewing.

Crawley proceeded across the camp to have a look at the Pen. The Dryhten appreciated the setting of the camp. The clearing was cut in the dense heart of the forest. Trees had sprung up all over the county in the last two decades but here was a real oak, not a quick-grow spliced with leylandii. It could have been five hundred years old and he had insisted that it be preserved in situ. It stood on the edge of a small knoll where it brooded like some cantankerous ancestral spirit.

And beside it was the Pen, where the subjects could be observed. He felt his own anticipation, how back in the castle room his fingers were gripped tightly on the arm of the chair. Very probably he was sweating. Slowly he would inspect each of the cells in turn. He already knew that all was well, but he wanted to linger, hovering on the edge of his achievement.

The North Downs were now forested so densely the road was almost dark. Ferns and undergrowth encroached and higher branches blocked sunlight so that Harper only saw the woman as he almost ran her down. He stopped the half-track, stuck his arm out of the cab and signalled for the convoy to halt.

Without speaking he motioned her up to join him in the cab. When she didn't move he lent out and had a look at her; she was carrying a small backpack and was dressed for hiking in boots and cords. She hunched as though trying to diminish the effect of her impressive height. She had long blonde hair tinged with silver. She looked in her mid-thirties.

"If you're hitchhiking," said Harper, "you're not very good at it."

She shrugged and smiled up at him without raising her eyes so that still he had not seen them.

"You should stick your thumb out," he said, "and nobody uses this road anyway."

She looked up and he caught the sting of the sea-blue gaze she gave him, then she looked ahead, taking in his own half track, Rahul's routemaster bus, the VW van and the Woolsey. "You use it."

"Oh well, we are nobody," he laughed as she took his hand in a trapeze grip and he pulled her up to the cab.

"Then there won't be any complicated involvements will there." Once again she let her eyes play across his face so that Harper, who wasn't easily embarrassed, blushed.

"My name's Harper," he blurted.

"Nice name."

"You have one?"

"Yes, I do."

He gave the signal for the others to follow. "Look," he said putting the half-track into gear, "this is not the place to be arsy with folk. You're in Kent now. They don't like snappy answers."

"Kent," she said, and lingered on the name, looking out of the window as the thick mass of beech and oak began to roll past them, "yes I've heard you can't be too sure of people round here."

"That's right."

"Then why'd you pick me up?"

"Oh," Harper said, flashing her his best devilish grin, "I can tell a rascal from their shadow."

"Well," she said and put her hand on his leg for a moment before brushing back hair from her eyes, "I'll take that as a compliment Harper. My names Mallory, Laura Mallory."

"Hello Laura Mallory. And what brings you to Kent?"

"Oh I'm just looking. What's your excuse?"

"Can't you tell? A half-track, an old London bus and a fine assortment of antique vehicles and strange folks with them. We're bringing the fair, juggling and hoopla with a bit of divination on the side."

"And what about tonight?" She put her head right out of the cab window to look above her, through the forest canopy. "It'll be dark soon."

"We'll pull to the roadside. Then you can have a bit of fairground folk hospitality." And Harper grabbed her hand, the hand that had touched him, and squeezed it. He was used to making a play for woman but there was something about this one. Laura continued to look out of the window, staring into the boughs and branches that criss-crossed like scribbles obliterating a page. When she finally deigned to notice his touch she merely lifted his hand gently back onto his own leg.

"We'll see," she said.

That night they sat around the campfire and listened whilst Rahul played "Paper Moon" on the guitar. There were too many names for Laura to remember: Jane, a dark-haired woman with a gaggle of kids; various teenagers juggling and a thin old man cosseting the spitted rabbit on the fire.

Harper decided he would impress Laura with his cartomancy. As she licked her fingers of grease he sidled up to her, cleared the ground of twigs and stones, and began to lay out his deck.

Laura watched with a raised eyebrow, the flames of the fire playing in her eyes and on her hair. "So you're a fortune teller Harper?"

"I have that gift."

"A gift is it? Don't tell me I'm to meet a handsome stranger."

"That's already happened." That line worked and she laughed and took the can of beer offered her. As she drank Harper put his fingertips onto the first of the cards. He felt the adhesion there, the gel creeping into the pores of his skin allowing him to connect with the higher reality, an inner space navigated by will alone. "This card," he said, "is called The Array or Infinity's Hall, it shows a room and on the wall of that room is a picture of a room, and on the wall of that room is a picture of a room...." He trailed off as the card pulled him in. It wasn't one that usually came up and he wondered now if he had ever truly understood it. The Array signified the higher realities that the cards themselves made available. How complex they were. You could enter the room with the picture then enter the room in the picture that it, in turn contained. Ahead were endless rooms stretching off in a series that made him dizzy. How casually we treat the infinite, he thought.

Vertigo overcame him as he imagined falling into an endless regression he could never escape from. The world became a series of trapdoors that opened into labyrinths of indecipherable symbols. With sudden insight he realised that Laura had emerged from this labyrinth.

"Harper," Laura said. He felt her hand on his arm, "Are you alright?" She laughed nervously and tried to make a joke, "Come back to me, come back to me."

Harper looked up from the cards, he wasn't in the mood for flirting, not now. "What does The Array mean to you?"

She shrugged, "None of this is real." Her eyes took in the trees, their encampment and finally the cards he had laid out.

"What do you mean?"

"These forests. They've only been here about twenty years. Mourne planted them as part of his great New Dawn. When I was a girl Kent was all fields; not strips like they have round the villages now but open land, stretching as far as you could see. But that was the result of man-made change too. Even if it took a little longer. Now your cards...."

"My cards?"

"They have an interface to a virtuality, yes?"

"The higher reality."

"That's just it Harper. It isn't. We treat so many things as though they're natural when they're not. The virtuality is like the forest; it was made by people."

Harper reached over and she let him take the can of beer from her. He had a long gulp and looked at his spread again. "The other main cards are The Portal and The Feast. The Portal shows a figure in silhouette attached to an old fashioned oracle."

"It's a virtual reality headset."

"So it has some significance for you?"

"I used to use one. A long time ago. They're obsolete now. As your cards demonstrate, nobody needs to wear a bowl on their head."

"You see there is something in the cards," but Harper knew that he was just playing the game now, performing a bit of showmanship because he didn't want to delve any deeper. In fact he wanted to pack the cards away, drink a lot more and sleep the whole night off.

"Well what about the last one?" Laura asked.

They both looked down at The Feast. It showed a medieval lord at his table, eating his fill with his courtiers. His wife stood at the side of the hall looking on with a bored expression. Meanwhile beneath the table huge maggots devoured a corpse. "It's not very nice is it Harper?"

"No," he said and he gulped in a breath, relieved that she didn't seem to be taking it at all seriously.

"I hope it doesn't mean that there are lots of creepy-crawlies round here." But it wasn't that she was taking it as a joke; rather she had realised something had disturbed him and was playing the child to put him at ease.

She grabbed the beer back and necked it as Rahul sang the final chorus of his song. "It's only a paper moon, hanging over a cardboard sea, but it wouldn't be make believe if you believed in me."

Over the next week they played the villages of the Downs, delighting folk who seemed to assume they were part of the Dryhten's twentieth anniversary celebrations. Harper, Laura and the others had all seen plenty of propaganda pieces about the new rural utopia but the people here did seem happy, if a little wary and out of touch.

Rahul would get the villagers hunting the queen or playing shell games; his punters marvelled at him since most had never seen anyone with dark skin. Jane ate fire, the teenagers juggled and performed acrobatics. Big Rondo the strong-woman held small children aloft in her giant hands. And Harper, of course, told fortunes.

They only ever stayed in one place for a day and were gone by twilight, onto the next small settlement and out of the way of any authorities that might get wind of them.

A few days before the main anniversary ball, Dryhten Mourne received a group of young intellectuals who had come to Kent in their enthusiasm for the New Dawn. The culmination of the evening was the performance of the skaldic storyteller. He stood before the fire and declaimed in alliterative verse the myths of the ancient Jutes. He spoke of the wars of gods and men and of those creatures that were neither: thusser, nisse, lund folk, ras, skogs and nok. To most of the audience these were words that, even in the recesses of their imagination, could find no shapes to fix upon.

As the convoy pulled out of the dell of Detling Laura sat beside Harper in the cab and stared out of the window as the forest enveloped them, cradling its branches over the dirt road.

"It's bigger than I thought," she said and as she turned to look at him he noticed her drained expression.

"What's the matter?"

"We've been travelling around for nearly two weeks now. I just thought I might have recognised something."

"You've been here before?"

"It's not that." She sighed and then, from her backpack, pulled out a notebook that had an old-fashioned screen readout. "Listen".

She started it up and played a recording. It was a young voice, a boy on the cusp of manhood. Full of life. "I am here at last, with other boys my age, all of us filled with and enthusiasm for the future we are helping to build.

"There's this brilliant old oak tree on a little hill, bark as rough as the skin of someone who's aged without any treatment. At night when I'm in my tent I can sometimes see its silhouette against the sky like a horror from one of those fairy stories you used to read me.

"Still we'll have the dormitories built soon and they'll let us use them whilst we finish our work here. Christen them for whoever's coming after us."

Laura's face was pallid with overworked misery. "There were others before that," she said, "with visuals, from the barracks in Canterbury where he was stationed. But once he got out, out to wherever it is, there was only sound. The last one I got was this." She pulled out a piece of paper, ragged where it had been handled so many times.

She read " ' I am writing this by hand! I didn't think they still carried these sorts of letters but you can piggyback them on the parcel service. They don't want any communication with the outside world but the word is that this project is very important. Close to the Dryhten's heart. It feels so great to be part of something glorious, something so much bigger than myself. At last I feel that I am contributing to the building of the better world that the Dryhten is creating.'"

Harper felt her gaze as he tried to concentrate on the road. He knew she was suffering but still felt a pang of jealousy for this missing lover. Laura had hooked up with them to find him that was all, not because she liked Harper. Yet she was now part of the fair, for whatever reason, and he knew that he could do nothing but help her.

They said little as the convoy pulled off the road into outer boughs of the forest and the fire was lit. She sat beside him and at last he turned and asked her, "So, this soldier, he was your fellow?"

"He was the same age as you Harper."

"What does that mean?"

"Look at me."

"I've looked at you plenty."

"Notice how my hair's got even greyer this last week, how the skin around my neck has sagged."

He hadn't noticed that. Just the sea blue of her eyes, just her laugh and the way her most mundane movements turned a dance that only he could see. He reached over and took a thick strand of her hair, held it as though its appearance here was as miraculous as that of a fragment of coral.

"It's grey," she said.

"Silver," he said, "beautiful."

"I'm nearly eighty Harper. I was a High Programmer in the Polity. Maintaining the virtuality."

He tried not to gasp. The opulence of the High Programmers was proverbial; they were creatures from a world he could hardly imagine, able to afford the best food and housing, the most effective treatments...."

"I had a juve job forty years ago. When I was still young enough to be vain. I could have had it renewed if I'd stayed. The hair is always the first to go. Then the skin. I might be covered in wrinkles soon."

He released her hair and he looked into her eyes, "Don't be so hard on yourself, lots of people use juve. Well, those that can afford it."

"So young and yet so charming," and she laid a finger on his lips in a proxy kiss. "He's called Robert and he's my grandson. Run off to join the Geoguth, the New Dawn youth-wing. I've not heard from him for a year. I even cracked the military records but there was no trace of him."

"We'll find him," Harper said, injecting as much purpose into his voice as he could. He stood up and looked around as though he was going to start searching immediately. Laura dragged him back.

They drank beer and some wine that the locals had given them until the fire burnt low. As the others bedded down they walked together into the forest to where they could hear the sound of a brook hop skipping over stones. When his skin touched hers she felt ripe and fresh. They rolled on the earth, in twigs and pebbles and the soft leaf fall from the autumn of a year before.

The next day they found the body. Just before they were due to strike camp Harper followed Laura as she went off to fetch water. He knew it was foolish to try and recapture a moment but when he thought of the night before he could not resist the attempt. What lover can?

He pictured her stooped beside the brook, hair dangling just above the surface of the water, her reflection cast by the sun between the islets of froth. But she hadn't got that far and in his hurry he almost ran into her.

"What is it?" he blurted.

Laura started, "You made me jump. It's...look."

She stood beside him, her hand finding his. The corpse was small, like that of an adolescent who hadn't quite finished his final growth spurt, and was dressed in a dirty loincloth. The skin was a smudged blend of green and brown with a texture like that of a frog. From its side blood had caked and dried from a wound that must have slowly drained its life away. Then Harper noticed the head and pointed.

"I know," said Laura without focusing because she had examined it at close range, had seen the pointed ears that were too large and the stunted nose that looked like a gnarled root. "But look at its back."

Harper turned to her. He didn't want to inspect the creature any further. He just wanted to be away from here. "What?"

"Go on."

He stepped closer trying not to glance at the body and understood why Laura had insisted. "It's beautiful." On the ground was what looked like a cloak of shattered glass stained with iridescent reflections from the broken rays filtering through the forest canopy. Little shards lay scattered about on the cushion of the forest floor like fragments of crystal. He noticed how a delicate frame tracery, like leaf veins, had held each tiny pane.

"If they were wings," said Laura, "I don't think it could have flown very far on them."

It hadn't occurred to Harper to fathom what he was looking it, he was simply drawn in by the play of light and colour. He took a step back inspecting the dead creature again whilst keeping a view of the broken wings behind it. Another step back and he was with Laura, looking at a dirty corpse that he did not understand. "What is it?" he said again.

"I don't know what to call it. There are no names here. If there was a name to describe this I'm sure it's in a language that's long dead. Or else it would be the coinage of some fantasist who'd never stumbled across the real thing rotting in a forest."

"Maybe," ventured Harper, "maybe it's like what you hear they used to have. In the fairs. Rondo tells tales about her grandfather's days, how they had a bloke with webbed feet. You know, a freak that could pull the crowds."

"I don't think this thing ran away from the fair. Do you? And one other thing," she bent down and lifted something from around the creature's neck.

"What?"

"Dog tags," she said, "it's wearing army dog tags."

On the morning of the anniversary ball the guests began arriving early filling the great hall, making small talk in anticipation of the Dryhten's entrance. He would call Rigby to dress him soon but he just had one more secret to savour.

Project Bestiary had been progressing so well that he commenced his inspection of it expecting nothing but good news.

As Harper and Laura emerged from the forest the other members of the convoy were being herded into the back of lorry by a group of soldiers. They were spotted before they had time to turn and run.

An enormous figure with huscarls's stripes waddled over to them flanked by a younger soldier. "You two. Where have you been?"

"In the woods," said Harper.

"See anything?"

Harper knew that neither he nor Laura had seen anything. He shook his head.

"What you been doing?" barked the huscarl whilst a prurient grin emerged onto the young soldier's face.

"I think he's got the idea," Harper pointed with his head as the soldier looked on the brink of giggling.

"Oh does he?" said the huscarl who now turned his attention fully on his charge and was on the brink of berating him when, from behind the lorry, an officer appeared. It was a thane wearing a beret emblazoned with a wolf badge. The huscarl immediately gave him his full attention with a "Sir."

"These two seen anything Huscarl Harris?"

"No sir."

"Well load them up then."

The huscarl gave the order to the young soldier and walked off with the officer. As he did so Harper heard him ask: "So you think we can keep it under wraps then sir?"

"Afraid not Harris. It just came over the communicator, the boss just went and paid a bloody visit didn't he. Spoke to him personally. Never thought he know so many obscenities."

Before Harper could even try to exchange glances with Laura, the soldier pointed his machine pistol at them both; his grey-green eyes blinking nervously beneath his forage cap. "Come on, come on," he shouted.

"You can't do this," said Harper.

"Just fucking move," he swept his weapon forward as though he could brush them along with it.

"Let's just do as he says," said Laura.

"What about our vehicles?" Harper asked as they reached the back of the lorry. The huscarl reappeared and poked Harper between his shoulder blades then grabbed the back of his neck and showed him the convoy. "We'll take care of that lad."

Harper saw soldiers moving down the length of the convoy splashing fuel from a jerrycan.

The Dryhten was determined that the ball should go ahead as planned. After screaming at the half-wit thane he took a calm-pill and tried to assess the extent of the crisis. The break out had only been discovered when the regular patrol had checked in after a full day out in the forests. By then the guards at the camp were all dead and the project staff themselves had been, not only murdered, but mutilated to such a degree that even the veteran thane had sounded disturbed. "They'd taken their time over them," he'd said, "done things to the features, as though they were trying to alter them."

All that could be done was to carry on searching and making sure that any civilians found in the vicinity were rounded up and debriefed. There could be no danger here in the castle. It was very unlikely that the escapees had retained much of their previous knowledge.

When the calm-pill had worked its magic he called for Rigby and began to dress for his grand entrance.

They had been in the lorry most of the day whilst it patrolled. Stopped. Went on. It was already growing dark when they arrived at the castle. As they came across the drawbridge Laura had seen a marquee surrounded by burning torches. People in elaborate costumes were milling around, drinks in their hands, laughing and joking. For a moment she caught a few bars of music. Then the lorry stopped and they were ushered out into a small dark courtyard and the whole scene had no more reality than a fleck of memory.

The courtyard was shuttered with a wooden gate and Laura heard it bolted. Soon she could smell the cigarette smoke of the guard duty on the other side. Slowly her eyes adjusted to the pale glare that washed over from some outside light source.

"I don't like this," said Harper.

Laura said nothing. She was trying to think. Fit all she had seen into a pattern.

"They're nervous about something," said Rondo nodding her head over to the gate and beyond.

"Yes," said Harper, "too bloody right they are."

"Shush." Laura touched Harper's arm. "Give me a card."

"Why?"

"I want to find out what's going on."

"But I didn't think you believed in it." Perplexed Harper pulled out his deck and dealt one off the top, not looking, not wanting to register any significance.

Laura held it in her palm inspecting it. "What is this one called?"

She held it close to his face. A young girl in blue with a headband tied around her fair hair stares into an ornate mirror. Instead of her reflection a death's head grins back.

"It's called <u>The Looking Glass</u>," said Harper.

"Well it'll do." She began to rub her thumb across the surface of the card feeling the adhesion of the interface. Then she was in. She confronted an image and knew that it was how she saw herself. The skin beneath her eyes caught shadows and her cheeks were lined with furrows. Was she looking that old already, that worn out? The card wanted to pull her into its dance of meaning, dangle mystic portents before her. She must try to see the underlying structures.

"You alright?" Harper asked.

She nodded, trying not to be distracted. Red Riding hood, Robin Hood, Robin Goodfellow, Goody Twoshoes. She admired Harper for his skill in interpretation. He managed to extract meaning from what was, to her, an overload of free-floating signifiers. Concentrating she isolated one image, a stick figure in black and white, focused on the area that held it and saw the cell of a data structure. It was an old database that seemed to be isolated, accessed only through Harper's cards. "Harper do you ever do general prophecies?"

"How do you mean?"

"Wars, disasters. Sad stories about the death of kings?"

"Well I can do...."

That was enough. Even this obscure little corner of the virtuality must have a connection. She looked around and found the death's head again, willed herself towards it. Where there was death there would be plague, war... yes. News.

From a general news server a simple search led her through a sun rune gateway to Kent. Government statistics. Ruralisation and resettlement. Triumph of New Dawn. Applications for various documents. This was public stuff but she quickly cracked though and found herself in the intravert, the closed system of Dryhten Mourne's regime.

She had been here before; had set out to look for her grandson Robert and fingered her way though military records finding no trace of him. She'd masqueraded as a medical sub-routine that checked inoculations and she tried this again, navigating through the records of every soldier making sure they'd had their jabs. Soon she found what she was looking for. Records for soldiers. All had serial numbers. Serial numbers that would appear on dog tags. But none of these soldiers had names.

Dryhten Mourne, dressed as Woden, surveyed the collection of visiting dignitaries, officials and admirers that had all come to his anniversary ball to pay their respects. He should have been full of self-satisfaction but he could hardly concentrate and found himself continually glancing off to the perimeter of the castle grounds to where the forest began. A large detachment of soldiers had been posted there all evening and, when last Rigby had reported back, all was well. His butler had been confused with the Dryhten's anxiety but that hadn't stopped Mourne sending him away again to fix up a makeshift sight connection with the thane commanding the soldiers in the forest. He had to know that all was well.

Rigby returned and discreetly handed him an interface which he let dissolve in his hand. Soon, over his immediate vision, he could see from the viewpoint of the thane. All was still and the men were arranged with their guns ready and with night-goggles that would flare at the slightest hint of life.

No matter how well camouflaged the portal to Project Bestiary was it couldn't keep out a determined woman with the skills of a High Programmer. She waded though a melange of mythological images cross-referenced with gene and morphological research. Then the details.

When she had seen all she had to, Laura disengaged and found herself back in the courtyard, gripping hard on Harper's arm and breathing in painful gasps. The card that was called <u>The Looking Glass</u> had fallen onto the cobblestones at her feet.

"What's wrong?" Harper asked.

"There were listed as raw material," she said.

"Who?"

"There were soldiers," she shook her head, "and they were listed as raw material. Don't you see? That thing in the forest, it had dog tags."

"I don't understand."

"I have to get out."

"What?"

"Please. You've got to help." She found herself pushing against the gate.

"How? The guards...."

"Please Harper. I think Robert is out there...."

Harper thought. "OK. We'll all go. At least you have a chance then. Rahul, Rondo, everyone! We're going over."

Once he had the constant assurance of a view of the forest the Dryhten began to relax again. Tomorrow he would have to make a measured assessment of Project Bestiary and work out what could be salvaged. It had been going so well until these recent developments.

As the band began to strike up again, the Dryhten allowed his attention to focus on the forest. All was still.

It was now time to make his speech, accompanied by music it would reinforce his vision of Kent. The music was rather plodding, too ponderous for his taste but the experts had insisted that it was authentic. In the distance he heard odd fumblings, birds and small mammals, soldiers fidgeting in their positions. There was an undercurrent, becoming louder. He checked the connection to the thane then remembered that it was only visual. He was hearing the sounds unmediated and they were louder now, infiltrating the stepped beat of the musicians. A scuttling, a squawk. Repeated. The guests were turning, searching for the source of the clamour. As the band stuttered to a halt there was a sudden and short burst of gunfire. He checked the thane's view and found him struggling through the forest in panic his night-goggles burnt with the blurs of rapid movement in infrared.

The guests were running towards the road leading to the drawbridge. The Dryhten was soon alone. He hardly noticed the chaos around him as he was concentrating on seeing what the thane saw. But the thane hardly registered the face of the creature that bought him down and rendered the connection useless.

The Dryhten stood in the deserted marquee. Slowly he took off Woden's great cloak and helmet; both now felt too heavy to bear.

"There seems to have been some sort of disturbance sir," said Rigby appearing from somewhere. "We should get inside." The Dryhten nodded.

As they trotted back he tried not to listen for the scurrying footsteps that he knew would soon be following. Even if they made it to the castle they would not be safe. Only the Dryhten knew the full extent of Project Bestiary, how his scientists had begun to bring the old stories to life creating a stage fit for heroes to stride upon. It was true that they had had to use some raw material and that had been rather unpleasant. But no one had suspected that the subjects would retain much information, that they might understand what they once had been and come in pursuit of those that had transformed them.

Laura ran towards the sounds, leaving the others to handle the guards, ignoring the flight of the costumed crowd from the marquee. She had wanted to escape into the forest to find other creatures like the one she and Harper had found; discover what they might know from the time before, when they had been enthusiastic young volunteers. Before they'd been snared in the twilight imaginings of their leader.

There was a burst of gunfire but this died abruptly. Then she saw them as they left the forest and came out of the night into the glow of the torches. Patchwork creatures thrown together from the order of all living things, some with insect wings, others cloven and fanged. They carried improvised weapons: branches of trees, a broken fence post. Some wore battered soldier's helmets and had rifles that they wielded as clubs. Out of their faces, textured like bruised fruit or tree bark, their eyes shone with the glee of the prey finally turning on their hunters. But what disturbed her most was that, even in a mob, there was still something human about each of them. A creature with an enlarged head that looked like a child giant stumbled on swollen feet and dragged the remains of a soldier behind it. A delicate, elongated figure crawled forward on stilt limbs like a crane fly. Laura held out her hands in entreaty as they came forward, searching their faces for a remnant that might be familiar.

Harper crossed the drawbridge just in time to see the hoard trample Laura beneath their hooves and talons. He started forward until caught in Rondo's arms and dragged into the shelter of the forest. They watched as the creatures entered the castle. Harper would only leave when he heard the first screams of slaughter from within. Then they turned and ran hoping the dawn would find them far away.

THE HEART OF THE LABYRINTH

There's this tape playing out, a scene that keeps repeating itself. There's this creature like a Minotaur rearing up and somewhere a baby is screaming.

"There's this tape," Helen said, "playing out in my head, a scene that keeps repeating itself."

She said it was always the same scene. There's this creature like a Minotaur rearing up and somewhere a baby screams.

A Minotaur. Or it's a goat. Or it's the devil.

The creature is only seen as darkness, a mass of darkness that could be a bushy mane or hair, perhaps part of the shadow is horns. The scream in the background might be a baby but could be something else.

"There's this tape," she said, "playing out in my head, a scene that keeps repeating itself."

It came to her perhaps twenty to thirty times a day by then; but she would not go and see a doctor.

"Remember what Rilke said: 'Kill all my demons and my angels might die.'"

But I did not understand what her angels were. And I was sick of listening. Even before she started all the there's this tape stuff she had begun to pale on me. Her endless discussions about art and her attempts to pry into what I was feeling. The next time she called I said I was busy. After that I screened her calls and didn't answer. There was another girl that I liked, a girl at work called Elaine.

Elaine was a small brunette, slightly chubby but I liked that. Helen had been tall and thin, with stringy blonde hair; not my type at all. By the time I got Elaine to come out with me Helen had stopped calling.

Me and Elaine went to the cinema in Islington and I walked back to Holloway Road with her, feeling her presence beside me, the tang of her CK One. We passed the window of the bondage shop with the dummies in rubber underwear, carrying whips, wearing masks.

"Kinky," I offered.

"If you like that kind of thing."

"Try anything once."

"Well," she said, "tonight you can have a coffee."

I had tea in her little flat near the Arsenal ground. I didn't try anything, we just talked about the film and I went home. I looked at the window display again, the poses of the dummy girl, bending over, pushing her arse out. For an instant a flicker of Elaine in the pose crossed my mind. Then my phone vibrated and I answered it without looking.

I listened to Helen's voice. She spoke carefully, taking her time, trying to stay in control.

"I don't think I can go on," she said, "I'm getting it more and more. Even as I speak there's this tape, playing out in my mind, a scene that keeps repeating itself.... I have seen doctors, but the pills don't work. There's just the scene, like a tape."

I went into Highbury Overground to go to her place, telling myself what a good bloke I was.

It was east and the train only took me so far. I had to get a bus, the only passenger, passing through grey streets beside canals and old factories. It was the sort of area where artists could get cheap studio space in disused warehouses. Helen's studio was high up in one of these places, up a steep stairwell.

When she opened the door she stared at me, squinting as though she had trouble recognizing me.

"Paul," she said at last.

Her eyes were rimmed and puffy, grey like the eyes in potatoes.

Inside everything had changed. Usually she kept her paintings in the studio bit at the back but now the living area had been invaded. The room stank of paint, and what I thought was thinners. Almost every wall surface was covered with pictures: her own and prints torn out of books or printed from the Internet. I recognized Picasso's Minotaur, images of Satan. Her paintings--with her usual signature distorted--were like nothing of hers I had seen before. Usually she did abstracts in pastel colors but these all showed the same image in dozens of variations: layers of darkness with the shadow of some indistinguishable form rearing up in the foreground.

On the coffee table was a half-finished bottle of scotch. She grabbed it and waved it at me.

"Drink?"

"Jesus, Helen," I said, "you've got to stop all this."

"Stop what?" she said pouring herself a large measure in a tumbler, "the excessive drinking? Or the descent into madness?"

From somewhere her face managed to form itself into a smirk and she slumped down into her armchair, her special armchair with the stuffing poking out of holes in the arms, the cushions.

I found a glass in the kitchenette and tipped some scotch in, just a nip really. I perched on the edge of the coffee table leant forward and placed my hand on her knee.

"You need help, Helen. I mean counseling, maybe a residential place."

She was hardly paying attention to me, staring into a space within. I thought of the words, there's this tape, playing out in my head. I needed to get her attention.

"Helen."

She drank some more, looked at me. She must be pretty smashed with all that scotch but it was hard to tell. Then she noticed my hand on her knee, looking at it as though it were some strange object she didn't recognize.

"Oh," she said, "Paul."

She grabbed my hand and pulled it forward, guiding my fingers to the inside of her thigh. I felt myself grow hard but I pulled back my hand.

"Is this what this has all been about?" I said, "you've got me over here to get back together."

"No," she said, "it just helps. Drinking helps. Fucking helps. Not much else does."

She stood, unsteady on her feet and came towards me. She thrust her crotch into my face and I could feel the shape of her beneath the skirt; I could smell her beyond all the paint, thinners and whisky. I ran my hands up the back of her legs and tugged her underwear. The glass of scotch fell from my hand spilling on the floor as I lifted her skirt to bury my head between her legs. She moaned, and all the while I continued with my tongue and mouth she was mumbling something, some sentence over and over.

Later we lay on the bed together and she reached out and held my hand. I let her hold it.

"It keeps it at bay," she said, "it keeps it at bay."

I recognized this as what she'd been saying.

"Helen," I began. I was going to say that I had to go now. Even though it was the small hours and it would be hassle getting back I wanted to be away from her.

"No," she said and I thought she had read my thoughts. But she slapped her own cheek with her free hand.

"I need to talk. To not talk about the tape. The tape in my head. The scene that keeps repeating itself..." she took a deep breath and squeezed my hand, her desperation cutting into my palm until at last she relaxed her grip.

"You remember what it was like in the beginning?" she said.

"What do you mean?"

"When we first got together. I used to love being with you. Just standing in an art gallery next to you I felt this sense of oneness, felt that everything was going to be all right."

She went on talking about the things we had done together, meals we'd had, parks we'd picnicked in during the summer months. She made it sound as though we had been together for years. What she was saying was as strange and unrecognizable to me as her talk about the tape, playing out in her head, the tape repeating itself.

As I was leaving in the morning, Helen mercifully asleep, I bumped into Galliano on the stairwell. He had the studio opposite. He was carrying some sort of shop dummy or maybe an artist's manikin.

"Long time, no see," he said

"Yeah."

"Back with Helen then?"

But I just shrugged and said see you later.

I missed work the next day. I knew that if I'd have gone in after the night with Helen, that Elaine would have recognized that I'd been up to something. And I really wanted Elaine. If the night with Helen had done anything it had confirmed that for me. I slept most of the day, switching off my mobile after I'd ignored the third call from Helen. The landline was already unplugged.

At work the day after, I watched Elaine through the glass partition that separated my office from hers. When she sat at her computer focusing on the screen her face took on a look of calm that was only occasionally disturbed by a slight furrowing of her brows. I would always study her carefully when she walked across to one of her colleagues, enjoying the way she carried her weight, the way she swayed. Once she saw me looking at her and smiled.

She didn't like galleries like Helen. She preferred to go to the cinema or eat out. I found I was staying more and more at her flat. It was a new build, white walls and shining steel fittings on the kitchen cabinet. It was as though it was an extension of the new Arsenal stadium which you could see from her kitchen window.

It didn't matter that I was staying there most of the time though in one respect. We still acted like we hardly knew each other at work. Or rather we acted as though we knew each other a little, as though we were just at the point of getting to know each other. The smile through the glass she gave. My studying her as she walked, as she swayed. These were acknowledgement of a distance between us that did not—I believe—really exist. If someone noticed her smile at me, coming through the glass barrier, they might think ah she's soft on him, when, in fact, only a few hours earlier my cock had been in her mouth or my snout nestled between her legs.

It was only after about two months that I began to wonder about her.

"Why can't we just let people know at work?"

We were never able to leave together, but would meet in some bar or cinema lobby or restaurant, usually near her flat. We rarely went to my flat because she said it was too near the office.

"I think it's important to keep a distance between your work and your personal life," she said.

When the spring came I took her to one of my favorite places: Victoria Park. There was something entrancing about watching the model boats on the pond, kids and their dads, old men with their remote controls in their hands, frowns of concentration focused on their vessels.

It was around this time that I came home to find a message from Helen on my landline. I thought she'd understood that it was all over, that I didn't want anything to do with her anymore. It was months since I'd seen her.

Paul, she said, just want to say that I understand it now. It's not what I thought. It's not what anyone thought. Take care.

It didn't really mean anything to me.

I'd never really thought much about mine and Elaine's relative positions at work. But then something happened to make it pertinent. Elaine was a line-manager for a small team of software developers. I was just a developer and although not in her team she was technically superior to me.

Then my manager went off sick, some immune system breakdown that meant he would be away for the foreseeable. Elaine was put in temporary charge of my team. The announcement was made by one of the senior managers. Elaine had come out from behind the glass partition and into our office. She was stood in front of us all, her small yet slightly chubby body was dressed in a checked work suit with a short skirt. I thought of running my hands over her and of the scent of her CK One. She avoided my gaze throughout the whole meeting until, at the end, when we were required to clap, she grinned at me along with everyone else.

We didn't meet that evening. She sent me a text to tell me she had to stay late to organize her increased workload. When we did meet, at the Greek Restaurant in Finsbury Park the next night, she talked a lot about work, asking me about members of my team.

I stayed at hers but we didn't fuck. She was tired and agitated about work. Wanted to get a good night's sleep.

The next evening I was at home alone when I absent-mindedly picked up the landline when it rang. I screened the call but didn't know the number. It was a voice I didn't recognize at first.

"Is that Paul?"

It was something about the way he said my name that made me realize. When I knew who it was I also knew what had happened.

"Galliano?"

"I'm sorry," he said, "I found your number on Helen's mobile."

She had jumped from the window of the studio. Apparently there was a letter for me.

"Give me your address and I'll send it," Galliano said.

"Yes," I said, Then added: "It's terrible."

"Yes," he said, "yes it is."

I rang Elaine. I wanted to go over, wanted to be with her, to be able to stop thinking about Helen. Helen lying on the rough courtyard outside the studio, her body broken. Helen taking the decision to open the window, to climb up on the windowsill.

"That's awful," Elaine said.

I took a cab over. I had to drink, to talk about Helen. Elaine listened, interjecting with <u>awful</u>, <u>terrible</u>, <u>poor girl</u>, in appropriate places. But I could tell she was tired. I slept on the sofa, confused about what I was feeling, not wanting to feel it anymore.

As always we went to work separately, me letting her go ahead so that I lingered in her flat, in the kitchen full of wipe-clean surfaces, of stainless steel door handles.

That evening Elaine was too busy to meet up. I went to the cinema on my own, hardly taking in the film. It was some action blockbuster, full of explosions and car chases. As much as I tried to concentrate, it seemed that the action was occurring in an order that made no sense, inserted in accordance with some algorithm for distributing such elements along the length of the movie reel.

The next morning the letter from Helen arrived.

<u>Paul. Don't worry, I think I understand it all now. Did you ever wonder why it was a tape? Why it was a tape playing? A tape playing out in my head, a scene that keeps repeating itself.</u>

There were several lines scored out after this. I could see what they were, a repetition of the same phrases, about the tape, the tape that keeps repeating itself.

<u>It couldn't be a DVD, which is more random, able to be accessed at any point. This isn't like that. It can only play in a set way. And I say this because even as I write this it is playing out, the same scene repeating…</u>

Lines crossed out.

Did I paint Minotaurs? Devils? I read about these things as though the dark shadow in the foreground could be identified. The Minotaur symbolizes the monster inside of each of us, so perhaps I was not too far off. But the darkness in the scene is not a Minotaur, not a devil. The scream, as I've said, could be a baby but it could be anyone. It could be me or you.

For a time, when I had really lost it, I thought it might be the government sending out signals, doing something to my mind. I almost became one of those people who wraps silver foil around their head to keep out the voices. I had to drink a lot then; had to go bars to find strangers to fuck; to it keep it at bay. But the drink always wore off and the strangers went away; they all had to get away.

I started to read about stuff on the Internet. I read about consciousness. You know there are scientists who think human subjectivity is an illusion, they call our feelings, and our discussion of our feelings, 'folk psychology'. It made me wonder if I had had some great revelation, that I was now experiencing a direct unmediated reality, where my thoughts could be seen for what they were: a tape playing out, playing out and repeating itself.

I read about other stuff. I'd started to believe I was in the presence of something evil, so I read about evil. But for evil to be a force it requires one to believe in an opposing force; to become trapped in the cat's cradle of faith. Then I read about humanity being alone in the universe, our insignificance. Of the universe not knowing, not caring about our existence. Of not noticing it. There was much talk of indifference.

But it wasn't the universe that was indifferent. How could the universe be indifferent? Indifference, to be something so positively malevolent, has to be human. It has to be what we do to ourselves.

I'll finish now. It has been an effort to write while all the time there's this tape playing out in my head. But sorry I've said that already haven't I.

Helen.

I told myself that I couldn't have made it turn out any differently, that she was mentally ill, that it was something chemical that the doctors should have treated; that she should have been looked after. But there had been a point when I hadn't really cared about her when I should have done. I didn't want to make the same mistake again.

When Elaine came out of her office the next day to talk about some work matter, I looked at her close hand, smelt her perfume as she leant over me. I told her that I needed to see her tonight.

"Shush," she said, looking around.

But she replied to the text I sent her later. We'd meet in one of our usual bars.

I bought flowers and waited at a table, not minding the grins I got from some of the customers, eyeing the blooms as they rested across the dark mahogany. I needed her to know what I thought about her, the way the relationship could go. We should be open at work, even if it meant me moving to another team or another office. It was time to get on with our lives.

I drank two pints while waiting, then got her text. I rang back immediately.

"What do you mean you're not coming?"

People in the bar heard me. I could see them smirking, looking at my bunch of flowers, at the scowl I was making into the phone.

But she was adamant. We would talk about it another time. Well maybe not tomorrow but soon.

I left the flowers on the table.

After Elaine told me it was all over between us a couple of days later, I promised myself that I wouldn't behave badly. I rang her a few times in the evening telling her that I'd really like to see her, that I thought things could be resolved. After a while she stopped answering my calls.

I still saw her at work of course. Every day she looked better. She had grown into the job, assuming a sort of swagger as she negotiated her way around the desks, her wonderful little body dressed in one or other of those professional suits with the short skirts she now wore every day.

When she spoke to me it was always about work. She used my name very precisely. Paul, she would say, I'd like you to have another look at this module. Or: Paul I think you need to re-do this. She grinned rather than smiled and she made sure her body never brushed against mine, or touched me in any way.

My evenings became a bit of a blur. I went to some of the bars that we used to go to; drank too much and thought about everything that had happened. I realized that I was waiting.

When it finally came I knew that it was not that I was being punished. Punishment would mean that something was paying attention to me when in fact I know that I had come to inhabit a vast indifference.

This morning I awoke hung over again. The curtains were closed and the light from outside was dulled by the heavy cloth so that I wallowed in shadow. I would not go to work today. I tried to think about what I should do but it was difficult. There is darkness in the foreground of my mind, a darkness that occludes thought. I see it form. See it move and somewhere something screams. Then it begins again. The scene playing itself out, over and over. Just like a tape.

ORIGINAL FICTION NOT AVAILABLE IN BOOKSTORES
hORRIFIED pRESS
WHERE FEAR LIVES !
Lulu.com
kobo
amazon
iBooks
Google play
horrifiedpress.wordpress.com